The Chance of a Lifetime . . .

"I have a little announcement to make," said Mr. Schwartz.

Everyone, including Liza's parents, looked at him expectantly.

"Lottya Zorinski is a dear friend of mine," he began.

"The famous drama coach?" asked Liza.

"The very same," said Mr. Schwartz. "I called Lottya last Sunday and asked if she had room for a Hyram Schwartz scholarship student at the Zorinski School. It's one of the country's finest private drama schools."

Liza's heart thumped against her chest. What was Mr. Schwartz getting at?

"If Liza passes the audition, then she has an all-expense-paid go-ahead to attend the Zorinski School," Mr. Schwartz announced. "She can start in December."

Liza was dumbstruck. This couldn't be true! All sorts of big stars had come out of the Zorinski School. It was practically a star-making machine. And Mr. Schwartz was donating a scholarship that could pay her way!

Everyone else in the room seemed equally surprised. For a moment no one said anything.

"Wait a minute," Mr. Velez spoke up. "Isn't that school in New York?"

**Look for these other books in the
SITTING PRETTY series:**

SITTING PRETTY
STAR MAGIC

by Suzanne Weyn

Troll Associates

Library of Congress Cataloging-in-Publication Data

Weyn, Suzanne.
  Star magic / by Suzanne Weyn; illustrated by Joel Iskowitz.
      p.   cm.—(Sitting pretty; #6)
   Summary:When she gets the opportunity to leave her small town to
attend an outstanding acting school in New York, fourteen-year-old
Liza is excited at the prospect but dismayed to be leaving her close
friends.
   ISBN 0-8167-2013-4 (lib. bdg.)   ISBN 0-8167-2014-2 (pbk.)
   [1. Acting—Fiction.   2. Friendship—Fiction.]   I. Iskowitz,
Joel, ill.   II. Title.   III. Series: Weyn, Suzanne.   Sitting pretty;
#6.
PZ7.W539Ss 1991
[Fic]—dc20   90-11151

A TROLL BOOK, published by Troll Associates,
Mahwah, NJ 07430

Printed in the United States of America.

10 9 8 7 6 5 4 3 2 1

For Ellen Steiber, with thanks for editing and guiding this series with such insight and caring.

Chapter One

Liza Velez dawdled at the front desk of the Palm Pavilion Hotel. She knelt and tied the laces of her white sneakers. Then she pulled out the bows and retied them.

All the while, her dark eyes were taking in the scene going on in the lobby. The technical crew from the daytime soap opera *Eternal Moments* had taken over a quarter of the hotel's lavish lobby. Three bright lights mounted on tall metal poles shone down on a small table and two blue-cushioned antique chairs. The table and chairs were set near one of the lobby's mahogany pillars.

"You'll sprain your fingers if you tie that sneaker one more time," said Samantha O'Neill, crouching down beside Liza. Sam's green eyes twinkled with laughter as she gently pulled Liza to her feet.

"Don't you even want to see what's on the assign-

1

ment board this morning?" added Chris Brown, joining them. Chris pushed some of her reddish blond hair back off her face and gazed at the soap set. "Wow! I can't believe *Eternal Moments* really came to the hotel," she commented.

It was Saturday morning, and the girls were reporting to their jobs as baby sitters at the Palm Pavilion Hotel. During the summer, they'd worked four days a week. Now that it was fall and they were in school, they worked on Saturday mornings and some afternoons after school.

Mrs. Chan, the assistant hotel manager, always tacked the day's assignments on a bulletin board. This morning, though, Liza hadn't even bothered to look. She was too interested in watching the taping of the soap opera.

"Can you go check my assignment for me?" Liza asked her friends. "I heard Philip Cruz and Lainie Bergman are going to be here. I don't want to miss them."

"We did check," said Sam.

"You're taking care of Jenny Majors," announced Chris, as if this were important news.

"Why is that so great?" asked Liza, not taking her eyes off the soap set.

"Jenny Majors just happens to be Lainie Bergman's daughter," Chris told Liza.

"Only Chris Brown, Miss Trivia Whiz, would know that," teased Sam, referring to Chris's love of movie and TV trivia.

2

"Really?" cried Liza. "I didn't even know she was married."

"Married four times," Chris said knowingly. "First she married her childhood sweetheart. Then a movie director. When they divorced, she went to a meditation ranch and ran off with her spiritual leader. After that didn't work, she married that super-rich guy Harry Majors. Jenny is their daughter."

"How do you remember all that stuff?" asked Sam.

"I just remember what I read in *Soap-Mania*. That's where I get all my soap trivia," Chris explained.

"What an interesting life she's had," Liza sighed.

"Interesting!" Sam shrieked. "She's been divorced three times! That sounds horrible to me."

Liza shrugged. "My parents are divorced. My mother seems okay."

"Would she be okay if she went through it two more times?" Sam challenged.

"I guess not," Liza admitted. "It was pretty tough on her. But celebrities seem able to handle it. Every time you turn around, they're getting divorced. Maybe they get used to it."

"Being in that business must be hard on marriages," Chris reasoned. "They're always away from home."

"Who cares?" said Liza. "It's such a great life.

You're rich, you travel, everyone makes a fuss over you. . . ."

At that moment, Lainie Bergman walked out into the bright lights. Her long, full blond hair shimmered. She wore a gauzy blue dress that was caught up with a clasp on one shoulder.

"She looks exactly like she does on TV," said Liza.

Next, Philip Cruz joined her. He was strikingly handsome in a beige jacket, with his longish dark hair swept back off his face.

"I guess their characters are going to run away together after all," Chris said. "I haven't watched since school started. But back in August they were thinking about eloping. I bet that's why they're filming down here in Florida. This must be their tropical love nest."

"If Mr. Parker sees us hanging out here, *we're* going to have to run away together," said Sam, referring to the hotel's strict manager. Mr. Parker had unbreakable rules about the staff bothering the famous guests in any way—rules that star-struck Liza had trouble obeying.

The girls walked over to the assignment board where they usually picked up the kids they sat for. Lillian, Sunny and Jannette, the three other sitters, were already there.

"Hey, guess what, Liza?" said tough-talking Sunny, tossing back her long red hair. "They're using maids and waiters from the staff to be in the scene over there."

4

"Uh-oh," said blond Jannette. "You shouldn't have told her that, Sunny."

Chris, Sam and Liza glanced meaningfully at one another. Jannette was a goody-two-shoes and a phony who had been in their class since grammar school.

"Why shouldn't she try to get into the scene?" said Lillian in her gentle West Indian accent. "It's a good opportunity for an aspiring actress."

"There's got to be a way," said Liza.

"Do not even think it, Miss Velez!" It was Mr. Parker. He had come up behind them, dressed as usual in his crisp sports shirt and Bermuda shorts belted high on his thin waist. As ever, his thinning hair was combed across the bald spot on top of his head, and he wore socks under his leather sandals.

"Why, Mr. Parker?" Liza asked. "Sunny said they're using staff. I'm staff. And I'm a talented actress. I really am. I could bring something extra to the role."

"Precisely my concern," said Mr. Parker. "They do not require a maid who bursts into song."

"Oh, I wouldn't—"

Mr. Parker held up his hand to stop her. "I have seen how you respond in the vicinity of camera crews, Miss Velez. I cannot have you menacing yet another production. Soon they'll stop filming here at all. And as movies are a great source of revenue and advertising, I feel compelled to safeguard these events from your zeal for the limelight."

5

"When have I ever—" Liza began to protest.

"I seem to remember you floundering in the pool in the middle of a Miles Lockhart movie."

"I tripped. That wasn't my—"

"I don't want to see you near the set," he said firmly.

As he spoke the children began coming out to meet their baby sitters. Jenny Majors was walked out by her short, balding father. She was a sweet little six-year-old, who seemed to have inherited her father's round face and dark eyes.

Sam and Chris also met with their kids. Sam was in charge of an eight-year-old boy named Troy. Chris had a seven-year-old named Hannah. The kids all wore bathing suits under their shorts. In no time, Sam, Chris and Liza were leading the children out to one of the hotel's three pools.

"So," Liza said, walking beside Jenny. "Do you always go with your mommy when she works?"

"No," Jenny told her. "Nanny takes me to school when we're in New York. My daddy is making this a vacation, so we came with Mommy this time."

"Are you having fun?" asked Liza.

"Kind of," Jenny answered, sounding unsure. "Mommy has been working all of the days. And at night she works on her lines."

"What about your dad?" asked Liza.

"He has business to work on. I get bored and I miss Nanny. My nanny is nice."

6

"You'll see Nanny soon," said Liza. *Poor kid,* she thought. *What good is having a famous mom if you never see her?*

The girls got the kids set up at the shallow end of the pool. Luckily, Hannah and Troy were nice kids. They included Jenny in their game of sea dragon and mermaid. Jenny got to be the little starfish, the mermaid's pet. This seemed to make her very happy.

Liza pulled off her staff polo shirt with the Palm Pavilion crest. Under it she wore a one-piece, jade-green bathing suit. She took a hair elastic from her shorts pocket and pulled back her long brown hair.

Sam and Chris were already in their suits. Liza joined them as they sat on the wide steps that led into the pool. "Can you believe that Parker?" she said as she stretched her long legs down into the water. "He acts like I'm some kind of menace to society."

"No, just to celebrities," said Sam, dabbing blue zinc oxide on her fair face.

"Someday when I'm a big star, I'll come back here and drive him crazy," said Liza. "I'll call him up and complain every second. I'll order champagne and send it back after I open it. I'll tell him the pool is too warm and I need the whole thing refilled."

"Chill out, Liza," said Chris. "It's not like the guy has ruined your life, or something."

7

Liza leaned back on her elbows. She closed her eyes and let the sun warm her face. "I can't wait to get out of this crummy town," she said. "If it wasn't for the Palm Pavilion, Bonita Beach would be nothing but a dinky little spot on the map stuck in the middle of nowhere."

"It's not that bad," Sam objected.

"It is," Liza insisted, leaning forward. "There's nothing here. There are no theaters. Only one movie. No museums. No decent restaurants. Nothing ever happens. I mean, look at this town. It's a few mini shopping malls and a bunch of seedy government buildings."

"There are some crafts shops. And some of the restaurants aren't bad," said Chris. "The Blue Dolphin, where my father works, is good."

"Okay. But those are only there for the people who come down to their vacation homes in the winter. And those people have lots of money. But face it, for people like us who live here all year long, this is a go-nowhere town."

"It's pretty," said Chris. "I like living near the beach."

"There are beaches in Hollywood," said Liza. "And in New York."

Sam had taken a flat beach ball from her tote bag. She began blowing it up. "Would you really leave?" she asked in between breaths.

"In a second," said Liza. "Most people who stay in

8

this town just wind up waiting on rich vacationers. I want to *be* a rich vacationer."

The morning passed quickly. The girls got into the water and played catch with the kids. They stopped for hot dogs and sodas at Sal's Snack Bar, out by the pool. Then they built a sand castle on the beach behind the pools. Before they knew it, it was two o'clock—time to take the kids back up to the lobby.

"They're still filming," said Chris, noting the strong lights still focused on the actors sitting at the table.

Mr. Majors came and picked up Jenny. "Your wife has a hard job," said Liza, nodding toward the set.

"Mmmmmmm," he grunted in agreement. He seemed annoyed that she was still working.

The girls met by the front desk when they were done returning the kids to their parents. "I'll be back in a second," said Liza. "I want to use the ladies' room before we leave."

"Oh, you mean the ladies' room that's right next to where they're filming?" said Chris skeptically.

"Is that my fault?" cried Liza. She began to cross the lobby. The truth was, Chris knew her too well. She didn't really need to use the bathroom. She just wanted to get one last look at the set and the actors before they left. They might be gone tomorrow.

As she passed she saw that the scene was temporarily at a standstill. A man, who seemed to be the director, was talking. "If we've decided they should be drinking in this scene, then I'll need somebody in a staff uniform to serve the drinks," he told a production assistant.

Quickly Liza pressed her palms down on the wrinkles in her blue shorts. "Excuse me," she called, pulling the elastic from her hair. "I couldn't help overhearing that you needed someone to play a waitress. . . ."

Chapter Two

Liza couldn't believe how quickly the hair and makeup people worked. Once the director okayed Liza for the walk-on role, a woman came up behind her and began briskly combing her hair. She clasped it into a ponytail with a lovely yellow bow on a clip. Without even saying hello, another woman applied base makeup, eye shadow and blush.

It had all taken only five minutes. Now Liza was standing to the side of the set, balancing a tray containing two iced teas with little umbrellas sticking out of them.

"Want me to say, 'Here are the iced teas you ordered'?" Liza asked the director, hoping to make the most of her small walk-on role.

"Don't say a word," said the director. He was a short, thin man who seemed to be in constant motion.

11

"I'll just smile then," Liza agreed.

"Just put the drinks on the table and get out of the shot as quickly as you can," the director instructed. "This is not the story of a waitress and her iced tea."

"Fine, no problem," Liza assured him.

"All right now, when Lainie says to Phil, 'I've always loved you' that's your cue to bring on the drinks," the director told Liza.

"'I've always loved you,'" Liza repeated. "Got it."

Liza looked over at Sam and Chris. They were standing off to the side, watching. She smiled at them.

They smiled back, but their smiles were nervous, worried ones. She knew they thought she was taking a big chance by ignoring Mr. Parker's rule. *Well, what if I am?* she thought defiantly. *I'll never get into show business by being timid.*

"Ready on the set," called the director. The actors took their seats under the hot lights. "Everyone ready?" the director continued. Liza took a deep breath to stop her hands from shaking. She had to seem calm and confident. "All right then," said the director. "Roll—"

"Pardon me." A familiar voice interrupted the director. Liza froze.

It was Mr. Parker.

"Yes?" the director inquired irritably.

"I hate to upset the proceedings, but I believe Miss Velez is too young to portray a waitress," said

Mr. Parker, staring icily at Liza. "I would hate for anyone to get the impression that the Palm allows underage workers to serve alcohol."

"It's just iced tea," the director protested.

"Nonetheless, it comes from the bar. Our real waiters and waitresses are all of legal drinking age. I'd be glad to send you a more suitable waitress."

"Fine, fine," the director growled. "But I'm already paying these people overtime. Get me another waitress, pronto."

"I will," said Mr. Parker. "And please forgive the interruption."

A production assistant whisked the tray of iced tea from Liza's hand. The hairdresser unclipped the bright bow she'd put into Liza's ponytail.

Liza stood there, trying to brace herself for Mr. Parker's fury. He came toward her and took her elbow, gently drawing her away from the soap-opera set. Her heart was pounding. When Mr. Parker was this calm, it was always bad news.

"Have we met?" Mr. Parker asked in a tone of complete seriousness.

Uh-oh, thought Liza. *He's finally flipped out. I've pushed him over the edge this time.*

"I'm sorry, Mr. Parker—" Liza began.

"You do know me then," said Mr. Parker.

"Of course, I know you," Liza replied. She looked past his shoulder for Sam and Chris. They were over by the front desk, pretending not to notice what was going on. How could she signal them that Mr. Parker had lost his mind?

"Then you *are* Liza Velez," Mr. Parker confirmed. Liza nodded.

"No," said Mr. Parker. "You're not. I must believe that you are Liza's evil twin sister. I must believe that, because I cannot believe that Liza Velez would go ahead and do this after the rather extensive conversation we had on the subject, just this very morning."

"Mr. Parker, I can explain. I didn't plan to—"

"No, you are most decidedly another girl. If I thought you were Liza I would be extremely upset. And I cannot afford to be upset. I have to supervise the Chamber of Commerce dinner being held in the Oceana Room tonight. I have a nonfunctioning walk-in refrigerator that is now defrosting—among other things—a five-hundred-dollar order of lobster tails. The costly little tails are unfurling and going bad even as I stand here wasting precious time talking to you."

As Mr. Parker spoke, his pale skin became redder and redder. Finally he turned, and without another word he stormed away from Liza.

Her legs shaking, Liza stood there a moment, trying to make sense of Mr. Parker's words. What it boiled down to was that although he was furious, he was too busy to deal with her right now. *Whew,* she sighed with relief, realizing she was off the hook.

14

"Do you still have a job?" asked Sam as she and Chris joined Liza.

"Mr. Parker's eyes were practically bulging out of his skull," Chris noted.

"I still have a job, thank goodness," Liza told them. "But I'm not on TV."

Chris shook her head ruefully and patted Liza's shoulder. "You just don't know when you've been lucky. Come on, let's go home."

The girls punched out on the time clock near the employees' entrance. A few moments later they unchained their bikes and rode away from the hotel.

The day had turned overcast. A heavy grayness hung over everything. They rode down a dirt road, dense with tropical foliage, until they came out to a two-lane highway. They followed the highway through the downtown part of Bonita Beach. It had never looked so dingy to Liza.

A dry breeze blew fine dirt from the road up into Liza's face as she rode. She wiped her forehead and noticed that some of the heavy base makeup they'd applied on the set had smeared onto the back of her hand.

The girls turned off the highway to the residential part of Bonita Beach. Chris was the first to reach home. She drove up the driveway of a small, neat yellow house.

Liza and Sam rode on to a corner where they each went their separate ways. "You seem pretty down,"

Sam observed when they had stopped for a moment at the corner.

"I guess I am," said Liza. "What happened today makes me wonder if I'll ever get to be an actress. Why wasn't I lucky enough to be born in Hollywood or New York?"

"When you're older you'll just have to go there," said Sam encouragingly.

"I suppose," Liza agreed. "Only, it seems such a long time to have to wait."

"That's because it is," Sam said with a smile. "But what's your hurry? You won't even be eighteen for another four years. You have time."

"I suppose," said Liza glumly. She pushed off on her bike and soon she was in front of her white stucco house.

Her mother stood on the lawn in her shorts, watering the scrubby flowers that bordered the house. When she was in her nurse's uniform, Mrs. Velez always wore her long, dark hair in a French braid. Now, with her thick, dark hair flowing loose down her back, she looked like an older, slightly heavier version of Liza.

"Hi, sweetheart," she called to her daughter.

"Hi, Mom," said Liza, coming up the walk.

"Listen, can you watch the boys for me?" her mother asked, referring to Liza's seven-year-old twin brothers. "I want to go down to Myer's Supermarket and pick up a few things for Thanksgiving dinner."

16

"Thanksgiving isn't until Thursday," Liza protested. She wasn't in the mood for Hal and Jimmy today.

Mrs. Velez shut off the hose. "I have a heavy schedule at the hospital this week. If I don't do it now, it won't get done. I can be back in a hour."

"All right," Liza said grudgingly. "Who's coming on Thanksgiving?"

"I'm not sure," said Mrs. Velez. "Tia Constanza, and maybe Poppi Juan, if his back is okay." Liza hoped her grandfather's back would be all right. She loved him. He was warm and funny. On the other hand, she could gladly do without her critical Aunt Constanza.

"Is Dad coming?" Liza asked.

"He said he'd come by. I didn't tell him about Tia Constanza being here. Do you think I should?"

"No," said Liza. "Or he won't come."

Mrs. Velez sighed. "I hope he doesn't bring Grandma Maria," she said, referring to Liza's grandmother on her father's side. "Nothing personal to her, but it costs a lot to feed all these people. I'm taking money out of savings for this meal."

Mrs. Velez got into her old hatchback car as Liza went into the house.

The twins lay sprawled in front of the living-room TV watching a Chinese martial arts movie. Totally absorbed, they didn't even look up as she passed.

Liza made her way to her small bedroom where

17

the walls were papered with posters of her favorite stars. Pulling off her sneakers and socks, she plopped down on the bed. The faces of the stars smiled down at her.

It was so easy to picture herself on one of those posters. Liza had known since she was small that she wanted to be a performer.

But would it really happen? Liza thought about her mother. Her pretty mother—who had wanted to be a singer when she was a girl. Now, there she was, worried about getting a turkey, worried about her fat, old aunt getting along with her ex-husband, exhausted from working overtime at the hospital to make extra money.

Her mother must have dreamed of a better life once. What had happened to those dreams? Why hadn't they come true?

"She's a prisoner of Bonita Beach," Liza muttered. There was something about the place that seemed to trap people. Maybe it was the heat. Perhaps it was the lure of lazy days spent on the beautiful beaches. She didn't know.

No, thought Liza, stretching out on the bed. *That's not going to happen to me. I'm getting out of here, no matter what.*

Chapter Three

On Sunday morning the phone rang at eight. Liza plodded, sleepy-eyed, into the kitchen to the yellow wall phone. Just as she reached for it, it stopped ringing, which meant her mother had it upstairs in her bedroom. She counted, "One, two, three . . ."

"Liza, it's for you!" her mother called from the top of the stairs. "Tell Chris not to call here so early on a Sunday morning!"

"Sorry," she called back to her mother. Liza had figured the call would be for her. Her mother's friends never called at odd hours like this.

It's her own fault, thought Liza, picking up the receiver. *I asked if I could have a phone in my room, and she said no.* If she'd had her own phone she would have gotten it on the first ring.

"Hi," she said.

"Hey, it's a beautiful morning. We're going down

19

to Castaway Beach," Chris spoke. "We'll come by for you in a half-hour."

Liza gave a wide yawn. "Can't," she said. "I have to be at the Palm at nine."

"Why? You're not working," said Chris.

"I promised Mr. Schwartz I'd play checkers with him for a little while. I'm meeting him at nine," Liza explained. "I don't know why he wanted to do it so early. I think Mr. Schwartz falls asleep in the afternoon or something."

"Is he paying you?" Chris asked.

"No," Liza said. "I was talking to him the other day, and I said I would play with him. Don't ask me why."

"That's so sweet of you," said Chris.

"I know. I'm hoping to be a saint someday," Liza replied drily. She was slightly embarrassed to be found out doing this good deed. Mr. Schwartz was a very old man who lived at the Palm. When Liza had first started baby-sitting in the summer, she was sometimes assigned to play checkers with him. If there were no kids to sit for, the Palm baby sitters were always asked to help where they were needed.

Now that school was in session, Liza, Sam and Chris only worked Saturdays and after school. Liza hadn't been assigned to play checkers with the old man since then.

Several days ago she'd seen Mr. Schwartz in the lobby. He'd stopped to talk with her. He didn't exactly come out and say he missed her. What he said was, "All the new daytime staff are fools who don't know the first thing about checkers!"

But, coming from eccentric, cranky Mr. Schwartz, that was as good as a compliment. And Liza knew it. Somehow—without fully meaning to—she'd heard herself volunteering to play checkers with him this Sunday.

"Well, when you're done, we'll be hanging out at the beach," said Chris.

"If you stay till twelve, I'll be there. I promised Eddie that I'd meet him," said Liza, referring to her boyfriend of almost four months, Eddie Moore.

"Okay. I hope you win at checkers," said Chris.

Liza chuckled. "You know I never win. Mr. Schwartz cheats. That's why he likes to play me so much. I let him get away with it. See ya later."

"Later," said Chris, hanging up.

Liza went to her room. She pulled a one-piece, blue cotton jumpsuit from her narrow closet and began to put it on. *I must be crazy to be doing this when I could be sleeping*, she thought. But deep down, she knew why she was going.

When she'd first met Mr. Schwartz, she'd called him the world's oldest, grouchiest man. Little by little, though, she'd grown fond of the cranky, old gentleman. And she knew he was fond of her.

The other reason she was going was that she liked talking with Mr. Schwartz. One day he'd revealed

21

that he'd been a stunt man in Hollywood and had even done a few small roles, mostly in westerns.

Back then he'd worked under the name of Chas Reynolds. He had a million stories to tell once he got rolling. Liza found his tales of old-time stars and the early days of Hollywood fascinating. Talking with him was like getting into a time machine and traveling back in time.

Liza grabbed a sugar donut and left a note for her mother on the kitchen table. Then she went outside for her bike. As she rode through town, Bonita Beach seemed quieter than usual. The stores were closed, and only the occasional car drove by.

Soon the glistening, rose-colored Palm Pavilion came into view with its crisp, white canopies flapping ever-so-slightly in the ocean breeze. No matter how many times Liza saw it, she could never quite believe it was real. It was so regal, with its palm-tree-lined drive. It seemed to her to be out of place here in ordinary old Bonita Beach.

Liza chained her bike and headed for the service entrance. Then she remembered she was off-duty. She switched directions and headed toward the white-canopied front entrance.

Pretending she was a wealthy guest, she passed the glistening indoor waterfall that cascaded down a wall of flat rock. In the lobby, two maids were vacuuming the rugs.

She stood and looked out over the lobby. For a

moment, she imagined that she had a pile of suitcases by her side. "Yes, porter, take these bags to my usual suite on the top floor," she imagined saying.

Then she would reach into a beautiful silk handbag and take out a fifty-dollar tip for the porter. "Keep the change," she would say. Liza had decided months ago that when she returned to the Palm as a rich woman, she would be an extravagant tipper. After all, she *had* worked here once, herself.

"Hi, Liza," a petite Oriental woman in a crisp blue blazer greeted her from behind the front desk. It was Mrs. Chan, the assistant manager. "What are you doing here on a Sunday? And so early!"

"Don't ask," said Liza with a laugh. "You wouldn't believe it."

Liza took a seat in the lobby. After a moment, Mr. Schwartz came toward her, hobbling on his cane. Every time she saw him, Liza was struck by his appearance. He was so thin, all bones. His soft shirts and pants flapped on him as though he were a scarecrow. Sharp cheekbones jutted out below paper-thin skin. And his dark eyes peered out with remarkable intensity. His thin, white hair wisped at the top of his head, adding to his flyaway appearance.

"Didn't think you were coming," he greeted her.

"Here I am," Liza said, getting to her feet. "I'll get the checkers."

"Hold up there," said Mr. Schwartz sharply. "I haven't had my breakfast yet."

"Oh, I'll wait here for you, then," she told him.

"Nonsense," he snapped. "You'll join me. Have you eaten?"

"Just a donut."

Mr. Schwartz rapped his cane on the floor. "How do you expect to play checkers on that kind of breakfast? Come with me."

Liza followed Mr. Schwartz into the elegant Oceana Room. The restaurant was a cool combination of blues and greens. Large watercolors of splashing surf decorated the pale green walls. Liza had often cut through the room on her way to the hotel's kitchen, but she'd never eaten in the restaurant.

When the waiter had finished taking their breakfast order, she noticed Mr. Schwartz staring at her. "What are you looking at?" she asked uncomfortably.

"I just this second noticed that you have a lot of Myrna Loy in you," he said.

"Who?" Liza asked.

"You never heard of Myrna Loy?" Mr. Schwartz barked. "What do you kids do, play video games all day?"

"No," Liza said in an offended tone. "I just never heard of Myrna Loy."

"All right, all right," Mr. Schwartz conceded. "But

Myrna Loy was a great beauty in my day. When I knew her, her hair was dark like yours. Later on, she lightened it. Never cared for that look on her."

"And I look like her?" asked Liza, pleased.

"You look like her some, but there's more. You have that same kind of sparkle she had. You knew she was going to be a big star even before she became one. It was written all over her."

"You see that in me?" Liza said, leaning into the table. Mr. Schwartz had met lots of stars. Liza was certain he was a good judge of star quality.

"Oh, you'll make it if you want to," said Mr. Schwartz, taking a cup of coffee from the waiter. "You have to really want it, though. You have to want it more than anything else."

"I do," Liza assured him as she sipped her juice. "Did you always want to be an actor?"

Mr. Schwartz shook his head. "I fell into it because it was work. I knew how to ride a horse, and I was young and foolish. I wasn't afraid to break a few bones doing stunts. The studios were always advertising for cowboy stunt riders back then. Once I became a stunt man, I got the bug. I worked day and night trying to break in as an actor. Only got but so far with it."

"You already lived in Hollywood, didn't you?" asked Liza.

"Yep. My grandfather brought his family out there 'cause he was panning for gold. He never

25

found any." Mr. Schwartz sat back in his chair and
laughed his dry, rasping laugh. "In fact, he lost all
his money. That's how my family wound up in
California. They couldn't afford to go back to Chi-
cago."

"See, that's the problem," Liza said, biting into
the French toast she'd ordered. "I have to find a
way to get to Hollywood."

Again, Mr. Schwartz studied her. "Would you
really leave your family and friends if an opportunity came along?"

"Sure," she said. "I mean, I'd miss them and all,
but I'd go."

Liza and Mr. Schwartz finished their breakfast
without much more conversation. Then they made
their way to the lobby and began playing checkers.

"You know, acting can be a lonely life," Mr.
Schwartz spoke up in the middle of a move. "It isn't
always, but look at me. Here I am all alone. I've
been married and divorced. I made a lot of movies,
but I'll be spending Thanksgiving all alone in the
Oceana Room."

Liza pictured the old man sitting by himself. It
didn't seem right that anyone should be alone on
Thanksgiving. "Why don't you come to my house?"
she said impulsively.

Mr. Schwartz sat back in his chair. "No, I
couldn't." He reached out and made a triple jump
with his red checker. "Well, maybe," he reconsid-
ered. "But you should ask your mother."

As it was, her mother had been complaining about the cost of the meal. Liza knew she shouldn't have asked Mr. Schwartz without consulting her mother first. It was too late now, though. She couldn't back out.

"She won't mind," Liza lied. "She loves having company."

"Then, maybe I will come," said Mr. Schwartz. "Give me your address before you go today and I'll be there."

At eleven, Liza said good-bye to Mr. Schwartz. As she pedaled her bike through town, she thought about what Mr. Schwartz had said. She'd have to find a picture of Myrna Loy right away.

Pulling up in her driveway, her thoughts shifted gears. Now she had to come up with a way to tell her mother that she'd be feeding one more person at Thanksgiving dinner.

Chapter Four

"You what?" cried Mrs. Velez when Liza told her she'd invited Mr. Schwartz.

"You always taught me to be charitable, and he's all alone," Liza defended herself.

"You're right," said Mrs. Velez, sitting down at the kitchen table. "I don't really think of feeding rich people who can afford to live at the Palm as being charitable, but—"

"But he's rich and lonely," Liza pointed out. "He's nice, Mom. Although he might not seem nice, he is."

"It's all right," said Mrs. Velez. "But you and I will have to watch the food. If it looks like there's not going to be enough, we'll only eat a little. Okay?"

"Okay," Liza agreed, planting a kiss on her mother's cheek.

The next three days before Thanksgiving were

busy but uneventful. Liza, Chris and Sam went to school, worked at the Palm and squeezed in beach time when they could.

Bonita Beach was busier in the winter. The mall parking lot was fuller, and there was actually a line to get into the town's one movie theater. The winter people from the north were beginning to arrive. By mid-December, Bonita Beach would be in full swing.

"Well, tomorrow's turkey day," said Sam on Wednesday afternoon as the three girls sat on a blanket at Castaway Beach.

"I hate Thanksgiving," moaned Chris, lying on her back, sunning herself. "Here I am trying to lose ten pounds, and everyone around me is pigging out. It's like I'm torn in half. I keep going back and forth. Food. Calories. Food. Calories. The food usually— no, always—wins."

"So, big deal," said Liza as she sat braiding her hair. "What's a couple of pounds more? Diet another day."

"Easy for you to say," Chris grumbled. "You never gain weight."

At that moment two boys came out of the water, surfboards under their arms. One was tall and dark-haired, with bright blue eyes. The other was shorter and muscular, with longish blond hair.

"Good waves today," said dark-haired Eddie, Liza's boyfriend.

"Not bad," agreed Bruce, settling down on the blanket beside Chris. He and Chris had been dating since the end of the summer. They were informally, casually drifting into becoming a steady couple.

"Look at that Lloyd go," said Eddie, gazing out at a lone surfer remaining in the ocean. "He never gets tired."

"He never gets tired of eating either," commented Sam. Lloyd was her older sister's boyfriend. He often ate at their house. "My mother went back to the store and bought another twenty dollars' worth of food when she heard Lloyd was coming to Thanksgiving dinner."

"The Surf Master must eat," said Bruce, referring to Lloyd with the reverence all the surfers felt for him.

"Hey, that reminds me," said Eddie to Liza. "Would it be okay if I came over tomorrow in the evening? There's nothing to do at my house after the meal is over. Unless you want to watch football, which I don't."

Liza threw her arms around Eddie's neck. "He hates football. Isn't he the perfect man?"

"He's touched in the head," cracked Bruce.

"No, he's not. He's too brilliant for that stupid sport," Liza replied. "Anyway, yes, you can come over if you promise not to eat. Not even a walnut. I already invited an extra person and my mother is nervous about the food as it is."

"I'm coming over, too," Chris invited herself. "I want to see how Mr. Schwartz does at your house. I can't picture him outside of the Palm. It's like, I imagine he'll evaporate or something if he leaves the hotel."

"I'll come with you," said Sam. "There's nothing happening at my house after supper, either."

"I hate to tell you this," Bruce teased Liza. "But I *won't* be at your house. I have to go to my Aunt Lucy's."

"Thank goodness," Liza sighed, rolling her eyes. "You're all welcome to come, but you can *not* eat."

On Thanksgiving morning, Liza rose early. She washed her hair and blew it dry. For the occasion, she used electric rollers, so that her hair curved past her shoulders in pretty waves. She slipped into a straight, short-sleeved cotton dress of cobalt blue. Liza liked holidays. They were a reason to get dressed up and look her best.

Liza made a salad, then helped her mother finish setting the table in their small dining room. They added the table leaves, which were usually stored in a closet, so that the table would be long enough for everyone.

At noon, the house was filled with the delicious aroma of roasting turkey. Poppi Juan arrived with Tia Constanza.

"Hi, Poppi!" cried the twins at the sight of their short, stout grandfather.

"¡Hola, muchachos!" Poppi Juan cried back.

Behind him stood Tia Constanza, smiling primly. She was really Mrs. Velez's half-sister, and was much older than Liza's mother.

"Hello, Liza," said Tia Constanza, offering Liza her cheek for a kiss. Politely, Liza brushed it with her lips. "My, my, what a nice dress," her aunt continued. "Are they really wearing them that short again?"

Liza clenched her teeth. This wasn't an innocent question. It was her aunt's way of telling her that she disapproved of the short length.

"Connie." Mrs. Velez swept in like a saving angel. "So good to see you."

"Hey, look at this!" cried Hal from the front window. Liza went to the window and looked out. A limousine was pulling up in front of the house. A chauffeur got out of the car and opened the back door. Out stepped Mr. Schwartz, looking elegant in a deep blue suit.

"That's my guest!" cried Liza, flying out the door to meet him.

"You look lovely, my dear," Mr. Schwartz greeted her.

"You look nice, too," she told him.

"Shall I bring your things from the car, sir?" asked the chauffeur.

"Of course, you should," snapped Mr. Schwartz.

The man seemed undisturbed by Mr. Schwartz's

grouchiness. He walked back to the curb and opened the trunk of the limo.

"You pay people good money, and you expect them to know their business," Mr. Schwartz grumbled to Liza. "Don't need them asking a lot of dumb questions."

"Is this your car?" asked Liza.

"I should say not," he told her as he hobbled up the driveway. "Rented it just for the day."

Liza helped him to the doorway. That was when she noticed the chauffeur coming up behind them, loaded down with boxes. "What's all that?" she asked Mr. Schwartz.

"You didn't expect me to come empty-handed, did you?" he asked, making his way slowly into the hallway. "Just a little fruit and what-not."

Liza was pleasantly surprised to see how Mr. Schwartz's presence seemed to make everyone come alive. With a stranger in their midst, her family was at its best. Even Tia Constanza lost her prissy expression as she attempted to make the old man feel welcome.

And Mr. Schwartz was a better guest than Liza could have imagined. To her great surprise, he spoke fluent Spanish. He and Poppi Juan laughed over stories that Liza couldn't fully understand, since her own Spanish was far from perfect.

When tall, good-looking Mr. Velez arrived with his mother, Liza's Grandma Maria, he immediately took to Mr. Schwartz. For one thing, the old man distracted Tia Constanza from harping on his faults.

Mr. Schwartz lavished compliments on petite, energetic Grandma Maria. Liza had never known Mr. Schwartz could be so charming.

The meal went by faster than any Thanksgiving dinner Liza could remember. Somehow, with Mr. Schwartz there, all the usual family tensions disappeared. And with the food he'd brought, there was plenty for everyone to eat.

"Would anyone mind if I watched a little TV?" asked Mr. Schwartz when they'd finished eating at four. "There's a movie on in which I played a small role. They only seem to show it on Thanksgiving."

"How exciting!" said Aunt Constanza.

"I was hoping to watch the football—" Mr. Velez began.

"Rick," Grandma Maria interrupted. "What is football compared with having the company of a movie star?"

The family settled around the set. "I don't come on until near the middle," said Mr. Schwartz, settling into an easy chair in the living room.

Liza turned on the set and found the right channel. Just as the opening credits began to roll, the doorbell rang.

"I'll get it," said Liza, hurrying to the door. It was Sam, Chris and Eddie. "We won't eat anything," said Chris as Liza opened the door to them.

"You can eat all you want," Liza said happily. "My mother's putting out dessert right now. Mr. Schwartz brought a ton of pies and cookies. And you're just in time to see this movie he's in."

Chris, Sam, Eddie and Liza settled down on the floor and watched the movie. It was a black-and-white western. Liza found the plot dull, but Mr. Schwartz kept things lively, telling interesting stories about the different actors.

"See that punch?" he said during a fight scene. "That fella really broke the other one's jaw by mistake. Held up production for weeks." He cackled at the memory. "That look of pain you see on his face is real."

About forty-five minutes into the movie, a dark, broad-shouldered ranch hand rode into the scene and announced that cattle rustlers had been spotted over a mountain ridge. "That's you!" cried Tia Constanza.

"Sure is," confirmed Mr. Schwartz, pleased.

"How handsome," commented Grandma Maria.

Mr. Schwartz laughed and stamped his cane on the floor. "Those were the days, I tell you!"

Mr. Schwartz appeared five more times, each time speaking a few brief lines. "That's it," he announced after the sixth appearance. "I'm not in it anymore, and I know how it ends."

"How thrilling for you to have been an actor," said Tia Constanza.

"Someday you'll have an actress in your family," said Mr. Schwartz.

"Yeahaaahhh! Liza!" cried Eddie.

Liza pushed him playfully, enjoying the attention nonetheless.

"In that regard, I have a little announcement to make," said Mr. Schwartz. Everyone looked at him expectantly.

"I wonder what it is," whispered Sam.

"Lottya Zorinski is a dear friend of mine," he began.

"The famous drama coach?" asked Liza.

"The very same," said Mr. Schwartz. "I called Lottya last Sunday and asked if she had room for a Hyram Schwartz scholarship student at the Zorinski School."

"Isn't that a private drama and arts high school?" asked Mrs. Velez.

"One of the country's finest," said Mr. Schwartz.

Liza's heart thumped against her chest. What was Mr. Schwartz getting at?

"If Liza passes the audition, then she has an all-expense-paid go-ahead to attend the Zorinski School," Mr. Schwartz announced. "She can start in December."

Liza was dumbstruck. This couldn't be true! All sorts of big stars had come out of the Zorinski School. It was practically a star-making machine. And Mr. Schwartz was donating a scholarship that could pay her way!

Everyone else in the room seemed equally surprised. For a moment no one said anything.

"Wait a minute," Mr. Velez spoke up. "Isn't that school in New York?"

Chapter Five

Chris found she didn't want to look at Liza or Mr. Schwartz. She stared at the plate in her lap and made a fork track in her key lime pie. The soft green pie was one of her favorite desserts. But right now she had no desire to eat it.

She wasn't fighting the battle of food versus calories. Somehow she simply wasn't hungry. *Lose one of your best friends, lose your appetite,* she thought glumly. *Well, it's one way to diet.*

Chris wasn't alone. No one else seemed very interested in eating, either. They were all crowded around Mr. Schwartz, asking him questions about the Zorinski School.

Liza seemed in a state of shock. Chris had watched her face when Mr. Schwartz made his announcement. Her brown eyes had grown wide and round as saucers. Her jaw had dropped. And her beautiful tanned skin had gone pale. She had looked from Sam to Chris to Eddie and then back to Mr. Schwartz. But she hadn't said a word. It was as if Mr. Schwartz's announcement was more than she could absorb.

Now she sat beside the old man, on the arm of his chair, listening to everything he said.

She still seemed to be in a dream, though. Chris could see she wasn't herself. There were no jokes, no wisecracks—only speechlessness and awed eyes. Chris had known Liza nearly all her life, and she'd never seen her this overwhelmed before.

Chris did have an idea of what Liza was feeling. She hadn't had to wait for Mr. Schwartz to answer Mr. Velez's question. She already knew the Zorinski School was in New York. As a trivia buff, she'd seen the prestigious boarding school mentioned many times in star biographies.

The school had opened in the sixties. Its founder, Mrs. Zorinski, stressed classical theatrical and musical training along with a strong academic high-school education. Its graduates showed up all over the place: on Broadway, in movies, TV shows, orchestras and ballet companies. A few had even gone on to become rock singers.

Chris knew that—if anyone was interested—she could probably give a long list of the famous Zorinski School graduates.

There was only one bad thing about the Zorinski

School. As Mr. Velez had pointed out, it was in New York.

Chris wanted to be happy for Liza. She had been—before she remembered how far away the school was.

"How are you doing?" asked Sam, joining Chris on the couch. She'd been over with the others listening to Mr. Schwartz talk about the school.

"I'm okay. Pretty surprising, huh?" Chris replied. "I'd never have expected Mr. Schwartz to do such a great thing. Aren't you shocked?"

"No kidding," Sam agreed. "What a great chance for Liza, though."

"Yeah," said Chris, her voice flat.

Sam shook her head sadly. "I know how you feel. I don't want her to go, either."

"She'll have to leave school and the Palm," Chris said. "And what about Eddie? Will they have to break—" Chris stopped herself and looked around. She hadn't seen Liza's boyfriend in the last ten minutes or so. "Hey, where is Eddie, anyway?"

"I saw him go into the kitchen," said Sam. "I wonder how he's taking this."

The girls went into the kitchen to find Eddie. He wasn't there, so they continued to the open back porch that led out into Liza's backyard.

That's where they found Eddie, sitting on the porch steps, his head in his hands. "You all right, Eddie?" Sam asked gently.

He looked up and smiled ruefully. "I'm just sitting here being a creep," he said.

Chris and Sam settled down beside him on the porch. "What are you talking about?" asked Chris.

"Here Liza gets this great chance, and instead of being happy for her, all I can think about is myself. I know I'm being totally selfish, but—it didn't seem to bother her for a second that she's going to have to leave me if she goes to this Zorinski School thing."

"I don't think she's quite realized all it will mean yet," said Sam.

"And if you're a creep, then so are we," added Chris. "We feel the same way. I mean, I've seen Liza almost every day of my life since I was six years old. I can't even imagine not seeing her every day."

"Me neither," said Sam. The three of them sat in silence, staring out into Liza's backyard. "Is this school really so hot?" Sam asked after a while.

"The hottest," said Eddie, who was interested in someday becoming an actor himself. "If someone offered me a chance to go there, it would be pretty hard to turn down. I don't know what I'd do."

"But it must be awfully competitive," Sam reasoned. "Liza will be in with kids who are all totally obsessed with performing all the time. You know how cutthroat and self-centered some theater people can be. It might get to be too much."

"It could," said Chris. "It might be too much pressure for Liza."

"I bet the regular education part isn't that great, either," said Eddie. "Suppose she decided later on to do something else besides acting? Then she'd be stuck with this crummy Zorinski-whatever education."

"Do you know for sure that the education isn't any good?" asked Sam.

"No, I'm guessing," he admitted. "But how can you have time for geometry when you're studying acting?"

"That's true," said Chris. "And she'll be all alone in New York without friends or family."

"Or boyfriend," said Eddie. "Don't forget, no boyfriend."

"Or boyfriend," Chris repeated.

"Though Liza would probably have a new boyfriend in a minute," said Eddie. "She's so pretty and funny."

"No, no, she wouldn't," said Sam, patting Eddie's shoulder. "She's crazy about you."

"You know," said Chris, getting to her feet, "maybe this isn't such a great idea after all. Liza is only fourteen. That's much too young to be away from home. It might damage her psychologically."

"It's definitely going to damage me psychologically," Eddie muttered.

"I'm serious," said Chris. "Liza is very sensitive. Who knows what effect a sudden change like this might have on her? I saw a movie-of-the-week where a girl developed amnesia when she left her home."

"I saw that one," said Sam, rolling her eyes. "Chris, she was running away from aliens who abducted her family. The creatures were so horrible she didn't want to remember them. That's why she had amnesia."

"Don't be so picky," said Chris. "The principle is the same. Unexpected changes can bring about bad psychological results. That's all I'm saying."

"She could be right," said Eddie.

"See?" Chris said to Sam. "We're Liza's friends. If we don't point out to her the drawbacks of going to this school, then who will?"

"Come on, Chris," said Sam. "Admit it. We don't want her to go because we'll miss her."

"That's not the only thing," Chris insisted, convinced she was right. "You can't just wrench people away from their home and expect them to be fine. People get all traumatized when they're uprooted."

"Great!" said Eddie, brightening. "When are you going to tell her all this?"

"Ummmmmmmmmm," Chris stalled, losing some of her zeal. "I don't know." She didn't want to be the one to burst Liza's bubble of happiness. Liza might think she was jealous and be angry with her.

"Hold on," said Sam. "We may be worrying over nothing. First off, she has to pass the audition."

"She will," said Eddie.

Chris nodded. "Liza is so talented. I can't imagine her blowing an audition. She's gotten the lead in the school play almost every year."

"Okay then," said Sam. "Here's another thing. We don't know yet if her parents will let her go. Mr. Velez didn't look all that thrilled with the idea. And you know him—he can be real stubborn once he sets his mind on something."

"You're right. He didn't look happy about the idea at all," said Chris.

"And we don't even know yet if Liza wants to go," added Sam. "She might decide not to, once she really sits down and thinks about it."

"I feel like a dope," said Eddie. "I mean, how dumb can I be, sitting out here worrying about something that probably won't ever even happen."

At the moment Liza burst out onto the porch. There was a happy light in her eyes. Her whole face seemed aglow with joy.

"Can you believe it?" she cried. "I must be dreaming. This is the happiest day of my life. New York City, here I come!"

Chapter Six

There was no school on Friday. Liza stretched luxuriously in her bed. She had nothing to do until two-thirty. Then she'd have to begin getting ready for work.

Yesterday's events played across her mind for the millionth time. The last person she would have ever expected to make her dreams come true was Mr. Schwartz. *Dear, sweet, wonderful Mr. Schwartz,* she thought fondly.

She knew her father didn't want her to go to New York—but she had to pray that he'd come around. Her mother said she could go if that's what she truly wanted to do. With her mother on her side, Liza figured they had a good chance of changing her father's mind.

Before the divorce, Mr. Velez had been a strict, even overprotective father. But now that he only came over some evenings and weekends, he seemed to have lost a lot of control over the situation at home. That was one of the benefits of the divorce, as far as Liza was concerned.

He'll let me go, Liza assured herself. *After all, it won't be costing him anything.*

Right now, she had a more pressing concern than convincing her father to let her go to the school. She had to convince the school representative who would view her audition.

Suddenly Liza sat up in bed. "What am I doing lying here?" she asked herself aloud. She had to begin preparing her audition. Mr. Schwartz had said that the rep from the school would be coming next week. That wasn't much time in which to prepare two acting monologues.

She threw a light robe over her cotton nightgown and hurried into the kitchen. Her mother was already sitting at the table, staring into her coffee. "You're up early," Liza noted. "I thought you didn't have to be down at the hospital until noon today."

"I couldn't sleep," said Mrs. Velez. The dark circles under her eyes were proof of her statement.

"Me neither," said Liza. "Oh, Mom, you don't know how excited I am. The Zorinski School. Imagine it! Mr. Schwartz said that casting directors always look there first when they need teenagers in movies. And kids who graduate are guaranteed to get into the best drama colleges. That is, if I'm not already on my way to stardom by then."

"New York is very far away," said her mother. "Are you sure you want to do this?"

Liza opened the refrigerator and stared into it. She didn't want to hear her mother's question. Yesterday, when Chris, Sam and Eddie had tried to ask her the same things, she'd changed the subject just so they wouldn't get the chance to voice these doubts.

"Of course I want to go," said Liza. *Okay, so I'm a little nervous,* she thought. *Who wouldn't be?* But to not go! What kind of wimp did they think she was? Not to go would be terrible. This was her dream come true. The chance of a lifetime.

Mrs. Velez got up from the table. "Cousin Frieda lives in New York now. I'm going to call her today and find out what kind of neighborhood this Zorinski School is in."

"Who cares about the neighborhood?" Liza cried.

"Your father does, for one. I promised him I'd find out."

Liza sighed loud and long. "You're both worrying too much."

"That's our job," said Mrs. Velez. "Once you're accepted, we are both going to have to talk with him. He's not at all convinced that this is a good idea."

"But I live with you now," said Liza. "Don't you get to decide stuff like that?"

"Who knows who decides what anymore," Mrs.

Velez sighed wearily. "He is still your father. If he's set against it . . . I don't know. Let's just wait and see."

Liza plopped down on a chair. Her father had better not stand in the way of her going. *He's got to say yes*, thought Liza. *He just has to. That's all.*

Liza finished dressing and rode her bike down to the small Bonita Beach library next to the post office. She wanted to find some plays for her audition. Although she had lots of paperback plays lying under her bed, she wanted something new. Something spectacular that would make her talent shine.

"One funny and one sad," she decided as she stood under the section marked Drama. She piled her arms with as many books of plays as she could hold, and then settled down at a table to pore through them.

When she found herself chuckling over a play called *You Can't Take It With You*, she decided to do the maid's monologue. It was very funny. Just the thing to show off how good she was at comedy.

She set that play aside and then began looking for a serious drama. It was difficult finding exactly the right one. Many of the roles were written for people who were much older than she was. She would feel odd trying to portray someone over twenty.

Liza searched through plays for almost two hours more. "This is hopeless," she muttered at one point. Then she found a play called *Look Homeward, Angel*.

Her heart started to hammer when she read the last scene of the drama. It was a monologue for a boy character who was about to go off to college to fulfill his dream of being a writer.

The scene was set at a train station. In it, the boy stood there, thinking about his family and the friends he was leaving behind. Liza blinked back tears as he spoke about the good times and the bad. *I can do this*, she thought. *With a few changes, I can make it into a girl's part.*

She got up and checked out both plays. They were perfect.

A rumble of hunger in her stomach made her check her watch. It was already one o'clock. She stopped at a phone booth and called Sam. "Don't come by my house for me," she said. "I'm already downtown. I'll meet you at work."

"We'll see you later," Sam agreed.

Liza rode her bike diagonally across the two-lane highway over to a small shopping arcade. She needed some lunch, and she knew Eddie was working at Flamingo Pizza there at the mall. She hoped he wasn't out on a delivery.

She chained her bike and entered the pizzeria. Bright pictures of pink flamingos decorated the walls. Liza smiled when she saw Eddie behind the counter. He had a black apron on over the official Flamingo Pizza Day-Glo pink T-shirt. He'd rolled up the sleeves, which showed off his tan muscles. Liza never got tired of looking at him.

"A slice and a root beer to stay, please," she said, smiling at him across the glass counter.

Eddie checked over his shoulder. When he saw that his supervisor was busy stacking straws, he leaned across the counter and gave Liza a quick kiss.

Liza's lips tingled at his touch. And she loved the way he smelled—part sunscreen, part pizza dough and part him.

"Johnny," Eddie called to his supervisor. "I have a break coming. Can I take it now?"

"Okay. Fifteen minutes," Johnny replied.

Liza paid Eddie for her lunch and took it to one of the pink booths. In a moment, Eddie joined her. She told him how she'd spent her morning.

"These two monologues will do it for me. I know they will," she told him as she ate her pizza. "Isn't this the most amazing thing that could ever happen to a person? I feel like it isn't real. Only it is. It's all going to happen so fast, too. Good-bye, Bonita Beach! Of course, Hollywood would be even better, since I really want to be in the movies. But New York is a great stepping stone." She drank her soda and looked at him. Eddie was usually very outgoing and expressive. Today she couldn't read his face.

"I'm going to do everything when I get there," Liza went on. "The first thing I'm going to do is see a Broadway play. I hear you can get half-price tickets on the day of the performance. There's also

50

off-Broadway, and off-off Broadway plays. It's like you could spend your whole life just going to plays. Not to mention movies. They've got theaters with Dolby stereo. I've never even *heard* Dolby stereo. I wonder what it's like."

She stopped herself. *All right, maybe I'm more nervous than I realize*, she admitted silently. Liza knew that she always rattled on, talking too much, when she was nervous. When she'd first met Eddie, she hadn't shut up for days.

"You say something," Liza told him. "I'm doing all the talking."

"I don't have much to say," Eddie replied. "How can I compete with Dolby stereo?"

"You don't want me to go, do you?" she asked.

"I do want you to go," he said. "You have to. It's a great chance."

Liza felt something funny twist inside her. "Don't you care that I'm leaving?" she asked in a quiet voice.

Eddie groaned. "Of course I care, Liza. But I understand what this can mean to your career. You know I want to be an actor. *I* would go if I could."

"You would?" asked Liza.

"Sure I would."

At that moment, a girl with long, dyed-black hair came through the door. Her name was Donna, and she was a grade ahead of Liza in school.

Liza detested her.

She was always hanging around Flamingo Pizza, making eyes at Eddie. He never responded, but that didn't discourage Donna.

"What's *she* doing here?" snapped Liza.

"Buying a pizza?" Eddie suggested.

"Don't be cute," said Liza. "What person our age goes around sitting alone in a pizza parlor eating pizza by herself? Kids hang around in groups, Eddie."

"How do I know why she's eating alone?" said Eddie. "Maybe that's how she gets her kicks. What's the big deal?"

"The big deal is that she gets her kicks waiting for you to notice her."

"Well, I'm not interested. Okay? So forget about her," he said, beginning to sound annoyed.

The girl walked past their table. "Hi, Eddie," she said. "Are you working today?"

"Hi, Donna," said Eddie. "Yeah, I'll be off my break in a few minutes."

"Good," Donna said, smiling. "You always cut the biggest slices of pizza. I'd much rather have you serve me."

Eddie looked down at his hands. "We all cut the same size slices. You don't have to wait for me."

"I don't mind," said Donna.

"Well, I do," snarled Liza. "Go eat your pizza. We're having a private conversation."

"Sorry, Donna," said Eddie. "We're in the middle of something here."

"No problem, Eddie," said Donna, heading to the front of the store.

"Is that why you don't care if I stay?" Liza asked. She rarely gave in to jealousy. But today she couldn't help herself.

"What are you talking about?" asked Eddie.

"You just said you wanted me to go," said Liza, getting to her feet. "Maybe you're more interested in Donna."

"I didn't mean I *want* you to go," said Eddie, frustrated. "I said—"

"Forget it, Eddie. I know what you said." Even as Liza spoke, she knew she was being unreasonable. Why couldn't she stop herself? "I have to go to work," she told him.

Without saying good-bye, Liza stomped out the front door.

Chapter Seven

At four-thirty that afternoon, Sam, Chris and Liza sat in the Palm's Oceana Room cutting shapes from scraps of felt. The three little girls they were sitting for—Jenny, Yvonne and Judy—made felt pictures by gluing the shapes onto paper.

The craft project had been Chris's idea and she had brought the materials from home. Mrs. Chan let them use the empty restaurant since it was closed between lunch and dinnertime. There were no customers, only the maids vacuuming and bus boys and girls setting up for the dinner crowd.

"The glue won't come out," Jenny told Liza, handing her the plastic bottle.

Liza took a bobby pin from the pocket of her shorts and dug into the clogged opening. She got the glue spout working again and handed it back to Jenny.

"How long are you staying at the hotel?" Liza asked the little girl.

"We're leaving tomorrow," Jenny answered, gluing a yellow felt sun onto her paper. "Daddy got a business call and now we have to leave."

"Too bad," said Liza. "I'll be in New York soon. Maybe we'll see each other sometime."

Chris and Sam exchanged quick glances, but they didn't say anything. Liza wondered what they were thinking. They seemed strange to her today—quiet, as though they didn't quite know what to say to her.

"I found two great monologues for my audition," she told them, trying to act as if everything were perfectly normal. "One is really a riot."

"That's great," said Sam as she continued to concentrate on cutting a piece of white felt into a cloud shape.

"When's the audition?" asked Chris.

"I don't know yet," Liza told her. "Someone is supposed to contact me."

They cut and pasted for several minutes more without talking. Liza kept thinking about Donna. Surely she wasn't Eddie's type at all. In her heart, she didn't think Eddie was interested in Donna. But she also knew that persistent girls sometimes got their way. And Donna was persistent. She'd been after Eddie since the summer.

"That stupid Donna was hanging around the pizza parlor again," she told Sam and Chris.

55

Chris chuckled. "From what I've seen, you know how to handle her."

"I had to tell her to get lost today," said Liza.

"You mean she came right up to you while you were talking to Eddie?" asked Sam. "That girl has nerve!"

"It was more like we were having a fight than talking," Liza said in a low voice. "It's extremely annoying to be interrupted while you're fighting with someone."

"The dream couple was fighting?" said Chris, amazed. Liza and Eddie never argued.

"It started out as a discussion, but then Donna came along. She just really bugged me more than usual today," said Liza. "She's so cheap-looking. Don't you think so?"

"Definitely," Sam agreed. "There's no contest between you and her."

Not even if I'm gone? Liza thought. How could she fight off Donna if she was in New York?

At five-thirty, they returned the kids to their parents. Lainie Bergman came to get Jenny. Her long blond hair looked as perfect as it had on the soap set. "Mommy, Liza is coming to New York soon," Jenny told her mother.

"Well, maybe," Liza said. She went on to explain about her possible scholarship to the Zorinski School.

"That's so fabulous," said the actress. "I felt badly

56

when you were bumped out of that scene the other day. But obviously your luck has changed. That's how it is in this business. It takes hard work and talent. But the rest is sheer luck. Either you get lucky or you don't."

"Can Liza come see us?" Jenny asked.

Lainie Bergman's eyes lit up with an idea. "You know, I'm always stuck whenever Jenny's nanny needs some time off. And she's had such a nice time with you here. Jenny really likes you."

The actress opened her straw purse and took out her business cards. She handed one to Liza. "This is my manager's number on here. He can always reach me. Call me when you get to town. Maybe we can work something out, baby-sittingwise."

"I will," Liza said with a smile. "That is, *if* I get there. I still have to audition."

"Remember to smile a lot and look your best. Personality and the right look can carry you a long way," Lainie Bergman advised, taking her daughter's hand. "Don't forget to call me. I can introduce you to some helpful people once you're in the city."

"I won't forget," said Liza, waving good-bye to Jenny.

Sam and Chris joined her. "I already have a baby-sitting job lined up in New York!" Liza told them. "With Lainie Bergman! I'm as good as on a soap already!"

"Cool," said Chris.

"You're sure on a lucky streak these past couple of days," added Sam.

"It's not luck. It's destiny," Liza told them.

"Whatever," said Chris with a shrug.

At that moment, Liza spotted Mr. Schwartz hobbling across the lobby toward her. She ran to meet him. "I want to thank you for a delightful holiday," Mr. Schwartz said to her. "It was memorable from beginning to end."

"I'll sure never forget it," said Liza. "I still can't believe what a great thing you've done for me."

Mr. Schwartz waved her off. "Thank me once you've been accepted to the school," he said gruffly. "I called Lottya and told her you're interested. She's sending a rep down to hear your audition next Saturday."

Liza drew a deep breath. "Well, I've picked out my monologues. All that's left now is to rehearse."

"Take a tip from me," said Mr. Schwartz. "Try to find a stage of some sort to audition on. The reps are used to it, and it impresses them more. Lottya told me that."

Liza twisted her hair around her finger thoughtfully. "I don't know how I could come up with a stage. Maybe the one at school, but the Glee Club uses that on weekends."

Mr. Schwartz rapped the floor with his cane. "I've got it. The hotel's convention center!" he said. "There's a nifty stage and auditorium in there."

"I don't think Mr. Parker would—" Liza began to object.

"I'll ask Mr. Parker myself," said Mr. Schwartz. Before Liza could stop him, the old man headed for the front desk and requested the hotel's manager.

Liza stood a few paces away and watched as Mr. Schwartz conferred with Mr. Parker. "What's going on?" asked Chris, coming up beside Liza.

"Parker's giving you the evil eye," added Sam. "What's Mr. Schwartz taking to him about?"

Liza told them. By the time she was finished explaining, Mr. Schwartz had returned. "All set," he told Liza. "You've got the convention room for next Saturday, and every afternoon this week for rehearsal."

"How did you get him to agree?" asked Liza, amazed.

Mr. Schwartz chuckled. "I told him if he didn't let you use the room, I'd book it myself and bring in the Bonita Beach Junior High Band to play all week."

Sam and Chris burst into laughter. "They are the worst! Do you remember when they played here for Civics Day?" said Chris. "If you could call it playing."

"They almost emptied the whole hotel," Sam said with a laugh.

"I remember," said Mr. Schwartz. "And so does Mr. Parker."

"I can't thank you enough times," Liza said.

"Thank me by getting into that school," said Mr. Schwartz. He yawned and checked his gold watch. "Nap time for me," he said. Seeming to forget they were even there, Mr. Schwartz walked away from the girls.

"He's a wild guy," commented Chris admiringly. "Weird, but wild. It's almost like he's your guardian angel, Liza. He's making everything happen."

"Figures I would have a guardian angel who looks like him," Liza said, laughing. "I guess it proves that if you can stand to play eight zillion games of checkers, something good will come out of it."

"I'll start practicing this afternoon," said Chris.

"We're going to swim down at the beach before going home," Sam told Liza. "Are you coming?"

"No," Liza said. "I want to go to the convention room and practice. I only have a week. Come to the auditorium when you're done. I'll go home with you."

She left them and headed for the convention room. She'd been there before. Back in the summer she'd landed a role as Miss Plucky Chicken, entertaining a room full of chicken salespeople who'd come to the hotel for a sales convention.

Pushing open the heavy door, she gazed into the dark auditorium. A dim orange light glowed at the end of the stage. It threw just enough light so that Liza could make out its T-shape—wide in the back with a long runway stretching out into the middle of the room. Metal folding chairs were arranged in rows all around the stage.

Liza stepped into the darkened room. She knew there was a light switch there somewhere. She felt along the wall for it.

Suddenly Liza jumped back, gasping. There in the dark she'd touched someone's hand.

Chapter Eight

"Good heavens!" cried Mr. Parker. "You startled me, Miss Velez."

"Sorry," said Liza. "Didn't you see me come in?"

"Apparently not. I was going to put the lights on for you, but I can't seem to locate the switch." He felt along the wall. "Ah, here it is." In a moment, the room was lit.

"So, Miss Velez," said Mr. Parker. "Mr. Schwartz tells me you may be leaving us."

"Maybe, but I'm not so sure I want to go."

There. She'd finally said it out loud. It was a relief to voice her doubt, but Liza was surprised to hear herself say it. And to Mr. Parker—of all people!

"Why is that?" asked Mr. Parker.

Liza shrugged. "All my friends are here. I've never lived anywhere else."

"Well, Miss Velez, I have witnessed the zest with

which you have pursued the theatrical life here at the hotel. Might I suggest that this is the acid test that will measure the degree of your devotion to a theatrical career."

"I don't quite know what you mean," admitted Liza. Mr. Parker's extravagant language often confused her.

"I mean that if you really do want to be a performer, you should seriously consider going to this school," explained Mr. Parker.

"You think I should go?" Liza questioned him.

"That is not for me to say," said Mr. Parker. "Allow me only to relate a story from my own experience. As a young fellow, growing up in New York City, I also aspired to the theatrical life."

"You did?" said Liza. She couldn't imagine stuffy Mr. Parker as an actor. She'd never known he was from New York, either. She realized that she knew almost nothing at all about Mr. Parker's life.

"I dreamed of being an opera star. I was told I had the voice for it, too." Mr. Parker sat down in the last row of chairs. His face seemed to soften as he spoke.

"I cannot begin to tell you the love I felt—and still feel—for the opera. *Tosca, Carmen, Rigoletto*. I would buy half-price tickets whenever possible. There, in that theater, I would be swept away by stories of passion and violence. The sets, the costumes! And, of course, the music. It seemed to me that opera singers must be more than human. Mere mortals could never sing as they did."

Mr. Parker's eyes took on a faraway glaze. He seemed to be seeing an opera in his mind. "There's nothing like an opera to put life into perspective. Here is real tragedy in its most heroic dimensions. All of life's small problems seem trivial when seen against the grand scale of an opera."

"Did you study to be a singer?" Liza asked.

"I was offered a scholarship to the Juilliard School," Mr. Parker said proudly. "That is one of the finest theater arts schools in the country. Oh, how I longed to join that elite group of opera singers."

"What happened?" Liza asked.

"My father convinced me that I would never be able to earn a living as an opera singer," he said quietly. "He had a point. For every great star like Luciano Pavarotti or Placido Domingo, there are hundreds of singers you've never heard of. Most opera singers are just happy for a place in a chorus, or a walk-on role."

Once again, Mr. Parker's eyes became clear and sharp. "So, I did the sensible thing. I studied hotel management in college and I've made a fine living at it."

"Then, it worked out okay for you," said Liza.

"Yes, it worked out okay," agreed Mr. Parker.

"So, then you're saying you think I shouldn't go to

the Zorinski School?" asked Liza, not quite getting the point of Mr. Parker's story.

"No, Miss Velez, that is not what I am saying," said Mr. Parker. "What I am trying to tell you is that it's been thirty years since I turned down that scholarship. And I still dream of standing in some chorus on a stage somewhere, singing at the top of my voice. A chorus job would have been good enough because I would be doing what I love."

"And you don't love running the hotel?" asked Liza. Mr. Parker seemed so devoted to the Palm. She had always assumed it was all that mattered to him.

Mr. Parker arched one eyebrow at Liza. "Yes, Miss Velez, I adore the Palm with all my heart and soul. But it is not an opera."

Clapping his hands together briskly, Mr. Parker got up. "That's enough of that," he said. "Be sure to turn off the lights when you are done rehearsing."

"I will," Liza assured him. She watched as he walked quickly out the door. Who would have dreamed that Mr. Parker had a beautiful singing voice? How very sad that he never got to use it.

Liza sat for a moment and thought about Mr. Parker. What must it be like for him to spend his life yearning for something that he would never be able to do? What did he think about as he catered to the many celebrities who came to the hotel? Did he still imagine—as Liza did—what it would be like to be one of them?

Only, for Liza, it was still possible. For Mr. Parker, it wasn't.

Liza took the *Look Homeward, Angel* script from her tote bag. She hopped up on the stage and began reading the words. Looking out into the rows of empty seats, she imagined an audience of faces staring up at her.

Then, slowly, as she read she forgot about the audience. She imagined she was at a train station in a small town. The train whistle sounded in the distance. Soon, the train would pull in. The train that would carry the main character, Eugene Gant, to his future, his destiny as a writer.

As she read, the words came out naturally. Her voice was strong, filling the room.

The character of Eugene Gant seemed to possess her. It didn't matter that he was a boy. They were both filled with the same longing—the longing to do great things with their lives. She understood him completely.

Liza read on. Eugene was leaving behind his girlfriend, Laura. Liza frowned. She would have to change that to a boy's name. What should she pick? Eddie?

Was she really leaving him? Or could they make it as a long-distance couple? Thinking about it made her chest feel tight. She decided to change Laura's name to Tom. It would hurt too much to use Eddie's name here.

Liza finished reading her lines. From the back of the convention room came the sound of applause. She looked up from her script and saw Chris and Sam standing in the back.

"That was great!" said Chris, walking toward her.

"Was it? Really?" said Liza. She knew she'd been good. But she wanted to hear someone else say so.

"I thought I was going to cry at the end," said Sam.

"Good. Crying is excellent," said Liza happily. "If you can make your audience cry, you've really touched them. I hope the person from the school cries."

"If you audition for the school rep the way you just did, you will definitely be accepted," Chris said confidently.

Liza jumped down off the stage. She looked at Chris and Sam. Their faces were like a part of her. A person couldn't ask for two better friends. They were always there for her. Always encouraging her.

"You guys don't want me to go, do you?" she confronted them.

"No, we don't," Chris admitted.

"But we want you to be happy," said Sam. "So, if you want to go—then we want you to go."

"Well, thanks," said Liza, suddenly feeling annoyed.

Wasn't there even one person who was going to cry and shout and tell her not to leave? Beg her to stay? Why was it so easy for everyone to let her go?

Chapter Nine

As soon as Liza got home that evening, she called Eddie. "I'm sorry I was so weird today," she said. "I don't blame you if you're mad at me. Are you mad at me?"

"Not really," he answered hesitantly. "I guess not." He sounded to her as if he had been mad, but her call had changed his mind. She was glad.

"You would never go out with Donna, would you?" she asked.

"Liza!" Eddie exploded. "No! How many times do I have to tell you that—"

"Sorry. Sorry," Liza interrupted him. "I just wanted to hear you say it one more time."

"If it makes you feel better, I think Donna looks like a vampire with all that dyed hair and eye makeup. I don't know how she can live in Florida and be so pale. I'd be terrified that she'd puncture my neck with her fangs if I got too close to her."

Liza laughed. That was one of the things she loved about Eddie. He had a unique way of always putting things in a funny light.

Two feelings hit Liza at once. She was relieved that they were friends again. But somehow, being mad at Eddie had made the thought of leaving a little easier. Now the choice was hard all over again.

Liza felt like her brain was going to burst with too much thinking. When she had problems there was one thing that always made her feel better. "I want to go down to the beach. Will you come with me?" she asked.

"It's going to be dark pretty soon," he pointed out.

"I'm going to ride down there anyway," she told him. "I just really need to go there. Don't ask me why."

"Wait for me," he said. "I'll pick you up. My brother isn't using his car."

No one was home at Liza's house. Her mother was working and the twins were at a friend's house. Liza quickly changed out of her Palm Pavilion polo shirt and shorts. She put on her flowered two-piece suit and covered it up with jeans and an oversize denim shirt.

After scrawling a quick note for her mother, she ran to the front door. She didn't have to wait long. In a few moments an old yellow convertible, covered with dents and rust spots, pulled into the driveway. Liza ran out and got into the car.

She threw her arms around Eddie. "I'm so glad to see you," she said. "You're glad to see me, aren't you?" She knew she was acting silly and insecure. But she couldn't help it.

"I'm here, right?" said Eddie. "Look, Liza, about today. What I was trying to say about you going away was—"

Liza put her hand over his mouth. "I don't want to talk about it. I don't even want to think about it. I feel like I'm going crazy. I just want to go to the beach." She took her hand from his mouth. "Okay?"

"Okay," he agreed. He started up the car and in a few moments they were driving toward Castaway Beach. They didn't talk. Liza gazed at the tall palms and the flowering trees. She'd been looking at them her whole life. Because she saw them every day, she'd stopped noticing how beautiful they were. There would be nothing like them in New York.

They passed through the Heights, the more expensive part of town. Most of the people in the Heights were seasonal. Liza had always dreamed that one day she'd come back to Bonita Beach as a rich star and buy her mother a house in the Heights.

If she didn't leave Bonita Beach, that dream would stay a dream. It would never become a reality.

Soon the old car was bouncing up a dirt road,

filled with gullies and pits. It was the road that led to Castaway Beach.

Eddie parked in the gravel lot behind the beach. He hadn't even taken the key out of the ignition before Liza jumped out and ran toward the water. She didn't know why she felt so impatient. All she knew was that at that moment she needed to be by the ocean.

The beach was empty except for the small white birds who ran back and forth at the shoreline, chased by the tide.

Liza stopped. And listened.

The crash of the surf filled her ears. She heard the pelicans as they circled overhead, looking for their supper. Their shrill calls were muted by the ocean sounds.

Eddie caught up with her.

"It's beautiful here, isn't it?" she said.

"Yeah, it is," he said. As he spoke he looked into her eyes. He seemed to be trying to read her, but he didn't ask any questions.

"I want to go to the cove," she said, taking off her sneakers. Castaway Cove was a sheltered spot to the left of the main beach. They walked along the shoreline until they came to a bend. When they rounded it, the beach became much narrower, and the water less wild.

Not many people came to the cove, but Liza loved it. She, Sam and Chris considered it their special spot.

Liza settled down on the sloped beach. Eddie sat beside her. He put his arm around her shoulders and held her tight to his side.

The sun was just beginning to set. Orange-gold light glistened on the crests of the moving water. The soft blue in the sky was slowly becoming streaked with a vivid pink.

"This is my favorite time of the day," said Liza. "It's not day and it's not night. I always feel that anything could happen in twilight. Even magic things."

"What magic things do you want to have happen?" Eddie asked. "If you could wish for something, what would it be?"

"I would wish to be two people," she answered without hesitation. "I'd like to split in two right now. That way one of me could go to New York to the Zorinski School."

"What would the other you do?" Eddie asked.

"The other me would sit here, like this, with you forever and ever."

The next thing Liza knew, Eddie was holding her tight and they were kissing. How could she ever leave him? She loved him so much!

"Tell me not to go," she said in an urgent whisper. "Tell me you won't let me go."

He stopped kissing her and held her face in his hands. "I can't."

Liza closed her eyes. "I know," she said sadly.

He lifted her chin and kissed her lips, and she returned his kiss. It felt so good being in his arms. He was excitement and safety, peacefulness and passion, all rolled up in one.

Why wasn't that enough for her?

She lifted her head and looked out to the ocean. The sun was now low in the sky. An ocean breeze lifted the ends of her hair. She stood and unbuttoned her shirt. "I want to swim," she told Eddie. "Want to come with me?"

"No," he said. "I'll wait here."

Stepping out of her jeans, Liza ran down to the water. It was warm and soothing as it lapped at her ankles. She waded in up to her hips and then plunged.

She swam through the dark, gold-flecked water, using all her strength. For a few moments, it almost seemed that she could swim to the setting sun that sat, fat and orange, on the horizon.

Then her energy lagged and she let herself float. Her hair drifted around her face like a mass of dark seaweed. For the first time since Thanksgiving she felt calm—at one with the world around her.

She was a coral reef. A school of fish. A wave. There was no need to make any choices. All she had to do was float there, rocked by the movement of the ocean.

The sound of a voice found its way to her. She lifted her head and treaded water. It was Eddie. He stood on the beach, waving his arm. His figure was a silhouette in the quickly fading light.

"Come on in," he called. "It's too dark."

Slowly she swam back to shore. Back to reality and to a world where hard choices awaited her.

Chapter Ten

On the Saturday of Liza's audition, Chris got up early. Liza had gotten the morning off from work, but Chris and Sam were still going in together.

Chris dressed and ate a bowl of cold cereal. In a few moments she was riding her bike over to Sam's.

Chris pulled up into the dirt driveway that led to Sam's small white house. The O'Neills' house was behind a larger one that sat close to the street. All summer and into the fall, the bigger house was empty. But now the shades were up, and she heard a radio playing at the kitchen window.

The people who lived there were winter people. They'd arrived for the season, escaping the cold northern weather. Soon Bonita Beach would reach its peak population—almost twice what it was in the summer months.

As she went up the path Chris noticed a woman

76

doing her dishes by the open kitchen window. The woman noticed her. "Hi," she greeted Chris, although they didn't know each other.

"Hi," Chris returned the greeting. For a moment, she wondered what the woman thought of her. Was Liza right? Did this woman see her as a member of some kind of servant class whose only purpose was to serve the vacationers? The thought hurt her pride.

Her parents weren't servants. They were educated people. And so what if her father managed a restaurant? That was a respectable thing to do. *And really*, she thought, *what was so awful about working as a maid? Or a baby sitter? You provided a service and people paid you for it. It wasn't as if they owned you.*

Liza is wrong, Chris decided. *This is a great place to live. And if vacation people help you to make money, who cares?* Chris loved Liza, but she supposed they would always look at things differently.

Sam's dog, Trevor, barked as Chris neared Sam's house. "Hi, Trev," said Chris, leaning her bike against the front porch. "Go get your master."

Seeming to understand Chris, Trevor jumped up on the screen door and barked into the house. "I'll be right there," came Sam's voice from inside. In a moment Sam came out, looking crisp and neat in her Bermuda shorts and a Palm Pavilion polo shirt. Her long blond hair was loose around her shoulders.

"You're early," she said, still brushing her hair. She checked her watch. "Almost a half-hour early."

"I couldn't sleep," Chris explained.

"I know what you mean," said Sam. "I kept thinking about Liza's audition all night, too."

The front door opened and out came Sam's sister, Greta. She looked pretty in her white cotton suit and flowered blouse. Beside her was a tall boy with white-blond hair. Like Chris and Sam, he wore shorts and a Palm polo shirt.

"Hi, Greta, Lloyd," said Chris. "What are you guys doing up so early on a Saturday?"

"The insurance office is open a half day on Saturdays," said Greta, who worked there as a secretary. "I'm dropping Lloyd off before I go."

"How do you like being the Palm's assistant pool manager?" Chris asked Lloyd.

Lloyd put an arm around Sam and scrunched her to his side. "I love it, and I have Sam to thank. It doesn't even feel like a job. You hang around, work on your tan, test the water temperature in the pool. Easy. I was made for the job."

"That's for sure," quipped Sam, wriggling out from under his arm.

"I do miss a certain amount of surfing time," Lloyd lamented, "but Greta and I are saving to get married someday. So it's worth it."

"My Lloyd with a real job," said Greta proudly.

"It does kind of boggle the mind," said Sam.

Lloyd and Greta got into Greta's beat-up blue Mustang. With a puff of exhaust smoke and a bang from the muffler, Greta pulled down the dirt drive. "Don't be late!" Lloyd called out the window. "Remember, punctuality is rule number one at the Palm."

"Is he joking?" Chris asked Sam.

"Hard to tell," said Sam. "He could be serious. Lloyd is super-into this job."

Chris shook her head and smiled. "I never thought I'd see the day Greta and Lloyd were going off to work together. I kind of always pictured them forever heading to the beach."

"It's bizarre, isn't it?" Sam agreed. "The flake twins enter the work force."

Sam sat on the porch step and finished brushing her hair. She pulled an elastic from her pocket and tied her hair back into a ponytail. Chris leaned against one of the porch supports. "Are you dying to leave Bonita Beach?" she asked Sam.

Sam leaned back on her hands. "Sometimes I am, and sometimes I'm not," she replied. "How about you?"

"I love it here," said Chris. "I would never want to live anywhere else. Does that make me weird?"

Sam laughed. "I don't think so. A lot of people love it here. I'd like to travel, though. I'm sort of like Liza, in a way. I have these big dreams. In the back of my mind I hope that if I keep working hard on my gymnastics, maybe someday I could go to the Olympics. And, of course, in my daydream, I win the gold and land on the front of a cereal box or something."

"I bet you will," said Chris. "I'll wind up staring at your face every morning as I shovel flakes into my mouth. It'll be good for my diet. I'll imagine that you're there saying, 'Chris, you don't need sugar on that cereal.'"

"Oh, great," Sam said, laughing. "I'm glad you'll always think of me as a nag." She looked up at Chris. "Do you have any dreams like Liza and me? I never hear you talk about any."

"I don't have any big dream," Chris admitted. "But lately I've been thinking that I'd like to be a marine biologist. I've noticed that I'm really happiest when I'm around the ocean and all."

"You could probably live here and get a job at the aquarium. It's only a half-hour drive from here," said Sam.

"Yeah, maybe," agreed Chris. "But it wouldn't be the same being here without you and Liza."

"Don't worry about me. I'll be around for a long time," said Sam. "I'm going to miss Liza, though. How can she just leave us? It's like she doesn't even care about us."

"I've been feeling the same way. It makes me sort of mad—but not so mad that I want her to go," said Chris.

"I'm not so sure she really wants to go," Sam observed. "She's been so quiet all week. And when was the last time you saw Liza be quiet?"

"The week she found out her parents were getting divorced," Chris recalled.

"Exactly," agreed Sam. "It's as if her body is here, but her mind is somewhere else."

"This may sound terrible," Sam said. "But last night I was actually wishing she would mess up her audition today."

"You were?" cried Chris. "I was, too. But she'll do fine. Last week when we saw her reading on the stage, she was great."

"And she's had more than a week to rehearse," added Sam. "I wonder why she wouldn't let us watch."

"She wouldn't even let Eddie watch," said Chris. "But at least they're not fighting anymore."

"Eddie seems real down in the dumps, though," Sam noted.

Mr. and Mrs. O'Neill came out onto the porch. Mr. O'Neill wore the captain's hat that he always wore when he took tourists out on snorkeling trips. A bright Hawaiian-print shirt was also part of his standard attire. "Time for another death-defying day on the open seas," he said dramatically.

He grabbed Mrs. O'Neill around her slim waist. "Kiss me, my love," he said.

Mrs. O'Neill laughed and kissed him lightly on the

lips. "See you at supper," she said as he walked toward his van.

"Mrs. O'Neill," said Chris. "Would you ever want to live anywhere else besides Bonita Beach?"

Sam's mother seemed surprised by the question. "I don't see why anyone would," she said, turning to go back inside.

"See?" Chris said to Sam. "That's how I feel."

"We'd better get going," Sam said, smiling. She went inside to get her large canvas bag. Then the two girls got on their bikes and headed for the hotel.

When they arrived, the Palm Pavilion was bustling. Each day of the winter season seemed to be busier and busier. Chris and Sam maneuvered through the crowded lobby and went to check the assignment board.

"We have two new kids today," Chris noted. Sam was sitting for a five-year-old boy named John, and Chris was assigned a four-year-old girl named Helen.

"Sunny and I are taking the kids down to the beach to look for shells," said Lillian. "Want to come?"

"Sure," agreed Chris.

"What about Liza? Where is she?" asked Lillian.

Sam explained that Liza had a three o'clock audition in the convention room. "You're kidding," said Lillian. "I can't picture the three of you apart."

"Neither can we," said Chris.

The afternoon went slowly. Chris wasn't used to spending so much time with Lillian and Sunny. They were nice, but Chris wasn't as completely relaxed as she was when she was alone with Liza and Sam.

At two-thirty—after a day of beachcombing, hide-and-seek and castle building—they returned with the kids to the lobby.

Chris stood with Sam and John waiting for John's mother to pick up her son. As they waited, Chris and Sam saw Mr. Parker escort a short woman in a black–striped jumpsuit to the convention room.

"I bet that's her. She must be the rep from the Zorinski School," Sam guessed.

Just then, Chris noticed Liza rushing through the lobby toward them. But there was something wrong! Chris nudged Sam and nodded toward Liza. "Look," she said anxiously.

"Oh, my gosh!" gasped Sam.

Liza was a mess. Her hair looked as if it hadn't been brushed. There were dark circles under her eyes. Her chin had broken out in a row of blemishes, and she hadn't even bothered to cover it with makeup.

"Are you all right?" Chris asked her.

"No, I didn't sleep all night. I'm so nervous I could die," said Liza. "I'm going to puke, I'm so nervous."

John put his hands to his cheeks and made loud barfing noises.

"Exactly," said Liza, noticing the little boy for the first time.

Sam took a brush from her bag and began combing out Liza's hair. "If you're going to puke, do it now," she told Liza as she stroked. "We saw the rep go into the convention room."

"Oh, no," cried Liza. "I have to get in there."

Chris took a lipstick from her pocket. "Here put this on," she said. Liza reached for the lipstick, but her hand shook. "Let me," Chris offered, applying the color to Liza's lips.

"I have to go. I have to go," Liza said. She simply turned and walked away from them, heading toward the auditorium.

"Boy, she's a wreck," commented Sam.

"I've never seen her like this," said Chris.

"Is she really going to puke?" asked John.

"I hope not," replied Sam seriously.

John's mother was late picking him up. "There she is," the little boy said after ten minutes of waiting. The woman apologized and took her son.

"Want to go watch Liza's audition?" Chris asked Sam.

"Yes," said Sam. "We can sneak into the back quietly. She won't even know we're there."

They went to the convention room and let themselves in as silently as they could. The back of the room was dark, but the stage was lit.

Liza stood on stage. She was doing the comic monologue from *You Can't Take It With You.*

"Are you having trouble hearing her?" Chris asked Sam.

Sam nodded. Liza seemed to be mumbling her words. There was a flat quality to her speech. And she lacked her usual sparkling stage presence.

The door opened and Chris saw Mr. Parker come in. He stood just behind them with his arms folded and watched Liza perform. "Oh, good gracious," Chris heard him mutter. "We must do something about this."

"Pretty bad, isn't it?" Chris whispered to him.

"Someone had better advise Miss Velez that she is bombing royally," said Mr. Parker.

"How can we?" asked Sam. "She's already in the middle of her audition."

"Hmmm," Mr. Parker reflected, stroking his chin. "There must be a way." Abruptly he turned and opened the door. "I will return," he said.

Chapter Eleven

Liza stood on stage, reciting the lines from her comic monologue. The voice coming out of her mouth seemed to her to belong to someone else. It was flat, low and emotionless. It was as if she couldn't find her own voice, and she was stuck with this other, inferior one.

She knew she was doing badly. Somehow it didn't seem to matter.

If she didn't pass the audition, it simply meant she wasn't cut out to be a student at the Zorinski School.

She droned on, and with every word she felt her dream of going to the Zorinski School slip further and further away. She knew the words by heart, but her mind wandered off the text. Instead of thinking about how the maid in the play would feel, she was thinking about not being an actress. For as long as she could remember, she had assumed she would act. Now she needed to think differently.

With a start, she realized that she had blanked out on the next line. "Ummmmm . . . ummmmm . . ." she stumbled. "I'm sorry, Ms. Clive," she said to the rep. "I really do know this. Just give me a minute to remember."

Suddenly the lights at the back of the auditorium were snapped on. "Lunchtime!" called a jolly voice. It was Mr. Parker. He walked down the aisle with a jaunty step. Behind him was a parade of three waiters rolling room-service carts with silver-lidded dishes on them.

What? Liza wondered. She walked to the end of the stage. "What's going on?" she called.

"I'm sure Ms. Clive here must be hungry," said Mr. Parker. "On the way in she told me her plane had just arrived not an hour ago. Didn't you, Ms. Clive? We all know how dreadful airline food can be."

Ms. Clive stood, looking as confused as Liza. "This is very thoughtful," she said. "But this young lady is in the middle of an audition."

"Surely you can't say that you are giving her a fair listening when all the while your stomach is yearning for food," Mr. Parker pointed out. With a flourish of his hand, he whisked the silver lid off the first tray of food. "Chef Alleyne's special avocado and radicchio salad, with his spectacular raspberry vinaigrette," he said as he revealed the large bowl of salad on the cart.

Ms. Clive's dark eyes took on a look of interest. "That does look good. And you know, I'm a vegetarian. They ran out of vegetarian plates on the plane. I didn't eat a thing."

"I knew you were a vegetarian," said Mr. Parker.

"You did?" the woman questioned him. "How?"

"The clear skin, sharp eyes, alert gestures. The minute you walked into this hotel I said to myself, 'There is a vegetarian, if ever I saw one.'" Mr. Parker walked back to the second tray.

Liza had never seen him this animated. His theatrical side was definitely showing. But what was going on? The other day—when he had asked if she was the real Liza—she had worried that maybe he was losing his marbles. Now she was absolutely sure he was going bonkers!

"Snapper almondine!" Mr. Parker announced proudly, displaying a white fish sprinkled with almonds and beautifully set in a circle of tropical fruit.

Ms. Clive looked at the dish, obvious longing in her eyes. "It's all very tempting, and very kind. But I owe it to this young lady to—"

"She doesn't mind," came a voice alongside the stage. Liza looked down and saw Sam standing there.

"What are you doing here?" Liza asked in a sharp whisper.

"Just a little moral support," Sam said cheerily.

When Liza turned back to Mr. Parker, he was gently leading Ms. Clive to a small folding table, which one of the waiters had covered with a white cloth and set with fine china. There was even a rose on the table. Clearly, Ms. Clive was allowing herself to be swayed by Mr. Parker's charming persuasion—and Chef Alleyne's gourmet cooking.

"Would you mind a short break, dear?" Ms. Clive asked hopefully.

"Not at all," Sam answered quickly for Liza. Before Liza could object, Sam had hopped onto the stage and was whisking Liza to the back.

Chris peeked out from behind the backstage curtain. "We can talk back here," she told Sam and Liza.

"What is going on?" demanded Liza.

Sam guided Liza through the opening in the curtain. The backstage area was dark and cramped. "That's what we want to ask you," said Sam. "What is going on with you?"

"What are you talking about?" Liza asked.

"We're talking about the fact that you are giving the worst audition anyone ever gave," Chris told her.

"Thanks a lot," Liza said drily. "I'm glad my fan club is here."

"Knock it off," Sam scolded. "We *are* your fan club. That's why we know you can do a lot better than you're doing out there. You sound half-dead. Even Parker could see that. It was his idea to interrupt the audition. *He's* the one who told us to talk to you."

"He did?" Liza questioned, surprised, yet touched that Mr. Parker was that interested in her. "You mean, he got all that food together for my sake?"

"It was pretty smart of him," Chris said, smiling at his cleverness. Then her expression grew serious. "He did it so that we could get ahold of you and tell you to do better. The Zorinski School is super-particular. You have to do your best."

Liza folded her arms stubbornly and turned away from them. "I am doing my best," she insisted.

"That's not true, Liza!" cried Chris. "And you know it."

Liza whirled back around to them. "It is true!" she exploded, throwing up her arms. "Something inside isn't letting me do better. It's like I'm all frozen up. I can't fix it. I don't know why."

"I know why," said Sam. "You're scared."

"I've been on stage lots of time. You know that," said Liza. "Being on stage doesn't scare me."

"I bet leaving Bonita Beach does, though," Chris said quietly.

Liza knew Chris was right. After all Liza's dreams and plans, she had to face the unpleasant truth: She was afraid to leave.

"If you don't do well at this audition, then the choice will be taken out of your hands, won't it?" added Sam. "You'll have no choice. You'll have to stay."

"I guess so," Liza admitted. "When did you guys get so smart?"

"We know you, Liza, that's all," said Chris.

"Think about it," Sam urged Liza. "Do you really want to blow this audition? Are you completely sure you don't want to go to that school?"

Liza sighed, covering her eyes with her hands. "No, I'm not sure."

"Okay," said Sam. "Go back out there and give a great performance. You can decide later whether or not you want to go. But then—no matter what you decide—it will be a *real* choice. It will be your decision."

"I don't know what I should do," Liza moaned.

"Do your best," said Chris. "Just think about the performance, nothing else."

"All right," Liza agreed. "I'll try."

Sam squeezed Liza's hand. "We know you can do it."

"Remember, you're star material," said Chris, patting Liza's shoulder.

Sam and Chris left through the opening in the curtain. Liza breathed deeply. She let all they'd said play in her mind.

They were right. She could decide what to do

later. Now the important thing was to give a good performance.

Liza parted the curtain. It looked as if Ms. Clive was still eating. She stepped back out onto the stage.

"There you are," called Ms. Clive. "Why don't you continue your audition? I can eat and listen at the same time."

She's already made up her mind about me, thought Liza. *She's decided I'm not that good. She doesn't really have to pay attention.*

Liza knew what she had to do. She had to change Ms. Clive's mind.

"I'd like to do my next monologue, the serious one," Liza said. "Then I'll start the comic one over again. That is, if you don't mind."

Liza thought she saw Ms. Clive wince, but the woman agreed to let Liza do it the way she thought best.

"I'll be doing the last scene from *Look Homeward, Angel,*" she said. "Eugene is standing at the station, waiting for the train. He thinks about his family and friends as he is about to embark on a new life."

As Liza spoke she knew something inside her had shifted. She recognized her own voice again.

And it had never sounded so clear and strong.

Chapter Twelve

"You are so unreasonable!" shouted Mrs. Velez.

Liza stopped in her front hall and listened to the sound of her mother's voice coming from the kitchen. There was no doubt in her mind whom her mother was arguing with. This was the fighting-with-Dad voice that Liza had heard so many times before.

"Why do you have to be so pigheaded all the time?" Mrs. Velez cried. *Slam!* She hung up the phone.

Liza was relieved. This was a phone fight. Since the divorce, there were more of those and fewer in-person arguments. That was good. Phone fights were a lot less upsetting to be around.

She walked into the kitchen. Her mother stood by the kitchen counter, still red-faced with anger. "What's the matter?" Liza asked.

Mrs. Velez poured herself a glass of water from the sink. "Your father makes me want to scream," she said.

"So I've noticed," said Liza. "What now?"

"How was your audition?" asked Mrs. Velez, changing the subject.

Liza brightened. "It went great. At first, not so hot. I couldn't get with it." She told her mother how Mr. Parker had interrupted. And how Sam and Chris had helped her turn her audition around.

Her mother smiled. "You have good friends."

"I know," said Liza. "Anyway, Ms. Clive said she'd have to let me know. But I think she really liked me, Mom. I heard her laugh when I did my funny monologue. I really think I made it."

As Liza spoke she was filled with new enthusiasm for going to the Zorinski School. Hearing Ms. Clive's approving laughter had filled her with new confidence. Giving such a good audition had been so satisfying, she wanted to have that experience again and again.

"Okay," said Mrs. Velez, sitting at the kitchen table. "We have a problem."

A cold chill ran up Liza's spine. "What?" she asked.

"Your father doesn't want you to go away to school."

"That's what you were fighting about?" Liza said.

Mrs. Velez nodded glumly. "If he insists, I can't go against him. He's still your father."

Liza was stunned. This was it. The thing she had been longing for. Someone was finally telling her what to do.

And it felt terrible.

"But that's not fair!" Liza cried. "He can't do that."

"He says you're too young to be so far away from home."

Liza dug into her tote bag and pulled out a brochure. "Ms. Clive gave me this," she showed her mother. "See, it shows the facilities and gives you all the information about the school. See how nice the dorms are? And they have an indoor pool. See, it's right there."

While her mother looked at the brochure, Liza produced more papers. "And she gave me these. They tell all about how the school tested academically. It's one of the top one hundred high schools in America."

"It does look nice," Mrs. Velez agreed. She handed Liza back the papers. "Go see your father. He's home now. Show him these. Maybe you can change his mind."

Stuffing the papers back into her bag, Liza headed for the door. She got on her bike and began riding to her father's apartment. *He has to change his mind*, she thought desperately. *He just has to, that's all.*

Mr. Velez lived in town, on the second floor of a

house next to a small shopping mall. In minutes, Liza was ringing his bell.

When he opened the door he didn't seem surprised to see her. "Come in, Liza," he said in his rich, deep voice.

"We have to talk, Dad," she said firmly. She walked into his neat, sparsely furnished living room. "You have to let me go to this school."

"Did you make it?" he asked.

"I'm pretty sure," she told him.

Mr. Velez ran a large hand through his short dark hair. He looked at her for a moment and then sighed. "I'm sorry, Liza. You're too young to be so far away from home."

"Cousin Frieda lives in New York," Liza coaxed.

"Cousin Frieda is a flake," her father said.

"She's a photographer; that doesn't make her a flake," said Liza. "Besides, I won't even need her. Every dorm has a dorm mother. You have to be in at certain times and everything. It's not like I'll be running around the city by myself."

"I've made up my mind, Liza!"

"Dad," said Liza, trying to stay calm. "Up until today, I wasn't sure what I wanted to do. Now I'm sure. If you could only know how wonderful I felt today when I was on stage! I was so good. This is what I was meant to do."

"Then you'll do it—when you're older," Mr. Velez insisted, beginning to sound upset.

"But this is the opportunity that will make it happen for me," Liza pleaded. "It will be twice as hard if I start out cold, without this training."

Mr. Velez shook his head. "There's no sense talking about it. I've given it a great deal of thought. You're too young. End of discussion." He picked his car keys up off the table. "I'll drive you home. I have to go out anyway."

"Mom is right!" Liza screamed. "You are pig-headed!"

Mr. Velez drew himself up to his full height of six foot three, and his voice became very quiet. "I think you'd better not address me in that tone of voice."

Liza burst into tears. Rushing past him, she fled out the door and down the stairs. "Liza!" he called after her, but she didn't stop.

Blinded with tears, she headed toward the mall. Eddie might be working. She needed a friend right now.

She ran to the glass door of Flamingo Pizza and looked in. There was no sign of him. Slumping back against the wall of the building, she let the tears run down her face.

They were tears of disappointment, anger and frustration. How could her father be so stubborn? For the first time in her life she wanted to hit him—pound on him with her fists until he changed his mind.

Wiping her eyes, Liza remembered she had to go

back to her father's apartment for her bike. But when she turned to go, she found herself face-to-face with Mr. Parker. "What are you doing here?" she cried without thinking.

"They do allow me out of the hotel from time to time, Miss Velez," he replied. "I even yearn for a slice of pizza occasionally." He studied her face quickly. "Can I be of assistance to you in any way?"

Liza was embarrassed. She knew her eyes were puffy and red. And at the sound of his kind words, she felt another onrush of tears about to begin. "No, there's nothing," she said in a choked voice. "Thanks, but—"

Liza cut herself short. Over Mr. Parker's shoulder she saw her father heading toward her. He was walking her bike.

She had to get out of there. She knew she would die of humiliation if Mr. Parker saw them fighting.

"I have to go," Liza told Mr. Parker just as a new flood of tears spilled from her eyes.

She ran down to her father. Since he had her bike, she couldn't just run past him. "Liza, would you calm down and listen to me?" he said. "I don't want you to be upset."

A flicker of hope sparked in Liza. Had he changed his mind?

"I'm doing this for your own good," he said.

Liza grabbed her bike from him. "No, you're not," she said angrily. "You're doing it because you're mean."

Getting on the bike, she rode off through the mall parking lot. She rode home crying all the way.

Her mother was in the living room when Liza burst in the front door. "Any luck?" she asked.

Liza didn't stop to answer. She was too upset. Her tear-stained face was her reply. "I guess not," she heard her mother say quietly.

Going straight to her room, Liza threw herself on her bed and sobbed. Now that she finally knew what she wanted, it didn't matter. She couldn't go.

All these days of worrying and wondering! And what for? Nothing.

Nothing! Nothing! Nothing! That's what her life would be now—thanks to her father.

When Liza's tears subsided, she lay on her bed looking up at the posters of movie stars she'd put all over her room. Would she ever appear on one? It didn't seem likely.

After what seemed like a long time, she heard the phone ring in the kitchen. "Hello," she heard her mother answer. "Oh, yes, Ms. Clive, how are you?"

Getting off her bed, Liza cracked open the door. Her mother looked at her apologetically. "Thank you," she spoke into the phone. "Yes. We think she's very talented, too. She'll be delighted to know that you've accepted her."

Accepted! She was accepted to the Zorinski School!

No matter what else happened, no one could ever take that away from her. She had been accepted to one of the best theater schools in the country. That meant she was really good. Not just good enough to have been the lead in the Bonita Beach Junior High play each year—but really, truly good.

"Before you go any further," said Mrs. Velez, "I have to tell you that I don't think Liza will be able—"

There was a sharp rap on the front door.

Who could that be? Liza stepped out into the kitchen.

Without waiting for a response to his knock, Mr. Velez walked in.

Liza sucked in her breath. What did he want? Had he come to scold her for being disrespectful?

"Excuse me," Mrs. Velez spoke to Ms. Clive. Holding the receiver to her shoulder, she faced Mr. Velez. "Liza has been accepted," she told him. "I'm about to tell them she can't attend."

Mr. Velez looked at Liza. "She can go," he said.

"Dad!" Liza cried. "Thank you! Thank you! Thank you a million times." She wrapped her arms around him joyfully.

Mrs. Velez's face lit up with a radiant smile. "Excuse the confusion, Ms. Clive," she spoke happily into the phone. "It seems Liza will be attending after all. Yes, you're welcome to come by this evening. Seven would be fine."

"What changed your mind?" Liza asked her father.

"I spoke to that hotel manager, what's his name?"

"Mr. Parker," Liza told him.

"That's right. After you ran off, he approached me and asked what the trouble was. He's an odd guy. Isn't he the one you always complain about?"

"Yes, but what did he say to you?"

"I told him why you were upset. He said he had been at your audition. He told me that one of the things you performed was very moving. He said it was one of the finest performances he had ever seen."

"Wow! I bet that was my *Look Homeward, Angel* one," said Liza.

Mr. Velez looked at Liza. He seemed to be studying her features. "Mr. Parker believes you have the spark of creative genius within you. He said to me—and these were his words—'If you do not allow that spark to ignite into glorious flame, you will be killing something very precious in her.'"

"He said that?" said Liza, touched by Mr. Parker's words.

"There was something about the way he spoke," said Mr. Velez. "For some reason I believed that he knew what he was talking about." Her father took Liza's hand. "I wouldn't want to kill anything inside of you. All I wanted was to keep you near and safe."

"I know, Daddy," said Liza. "But I will be safe. I promise."

"I asked Mr. Parker about that, too," said Mr. Velez. "I asked if he thought you were mature enough to deal with being away from home."

Liza cringed. That wasn't exactly a great question to ask Mr. Parker—not after all the times she'd gotten into trouble at the Palm. "What did he say?" she asked quietly.

Mr. Velez smiled. "He said you were a little zany."

"Zany!" cried Liza.

"That was his word, not mine," said Mr. Velez. "But he also told me he'd watched you with the kids at the hotel. He said he never had a moment of worry about those children. He knew you were responsible enough to take good care of them. In his opinion, that meant you were a mature young lady, despite everything else. . . . What did he mean by 'despite everything else'?"

"Nothing," said Liza. "That's just how he talks."

Mrs. Velez came over to her ex-husband and kissed his cheek. Liza hadn't seen her do that in many years. "Thank you, Rick," she said. "I'm sorry I called you pigheaded."

"You should be," he sulked.

"Me, too," said Liza.

Mrs. Velez gasped. "Liza! You didn't!"

Mr. Velez shrugged. "Like mother, like daughter.

It's a good thing we're shipping you off. I can't have two against one."

Liza hugged him again. "You're not shipping me off. I'll always be around to bug you."

"You'd better be," said Mr. Velez. And this time, there were tears in *his* eyes.

Chapter Thirteen

Ms. Clive came to Liza's house that evening and spoke to her parents. She had a video of the Zorinski School and its activities to show them. The school was more than Liza had dreamed. Part of it had originally been an old convent school. But there was a new wing—donated by a big movie director who'd attended the school. The new wing contained the indoor pool, a gymnasium, a large modern auditorium and stage and a cafeteria.

If Liza had any last doubts about going, the video wiped them away.

"Mrs. Zorinski can take you right away," Ms. Clive told Liza. "We don't usually take students at mid-session, but apparently your mentor, Mr. Schwartz, is a very dear personal friend of Mrs. Zorinski's. She speaks so highly of him."

Liza smiled softly. For all his cranky ways, it

seemed Mr. Schwartz had touched the lives of many people. *It's funny,* she thought fondly, *the way some people fool you at first.*

The next day, Sunday, Sam and Chris came over. They sat together on Liza's back porch. "I can't believe you're really going," said Sam.

"It's going to be weird not having you around," added Chris.

"I know," said Liza. "But I'll be back for two whole weeks at Christmastime. Then we get a week off for spring break. Then before you know it—it's summer, and I'll be back for two months!"

"But you won't be here every day," said Chris.

"I'll write all the time," Liza promised. "And there's always the greatest invention of the nineteenth century."

"The telephone!" Chris and Sam said at once.

"Exactly!" Liza laughed.

"My father is always having fits over the phone bill, as it is," said Sam. "Wait until he sees calls to New York on there."

"We're working," Chris pointed out. "We can pay for the calls ourselves."

"Maybe when I'm there I'll be sitting for Jenny Majors, so I'll be able to call you, too," said Liza. "It won't be so bad."

"Hey, maybe we'll be able to come visit you in New York sometime," said Chris.

"That would be so cool," said Liza.

"Have you told Eddie yet?" asked Sam.

Liza shook her head. "I'm going to do that today."

Sam got to her feet. "I have to go," she said. "We're all going out on a snorkeling trip. Just my family. Dad's into this family togetherness thing lately."

"I'll come with you," said Chris, heading down the porch steps with Sam. "I have a science report to finish."

"See ya later," said Liza. She went inside and called Eddie. "Feel like going to the beach?" he asked.

"Always," she replied.

He picked her up in his brother's old car, and they drove down to Castaway Beach together. Eddie had his surfboard stashed in the back seat.

The beach was busier than usual. The winter people were out in full force. Eddie had to park his car out on the road. "It's kind of funny, isn't it," he said as they got out of the car. "All those people from up north are coming here—and you're going there."

"How did you know?" asked Liza, stunned.

"When I asked how your audition went yesterday, you said, 'Okay.'"

"So what?" asked Liza.

Eddie lifted his surfboard from the back of the car. "So normally you would have told me what happened in minute-by-minute detail. If you hadn't made it, or if you'd decided not to go, you would have told me right away," he explained. "There was only one thing left for me to think. That you made it and you're going and you were waiting for a good time to tell me about it. I'm right, aren't I?"

Liza nodded. "You're right." She came around to his side of the car and stood beside him.

"Congratulations," he said. "I really am happy for you. You're going to love it."

"Does this mean we have to break up?" Liza asked him.

Eddie shrugged. "I've been wondering that myself," he replied. "Maybe we could just kind of hang loose and see what happens."

"I guess you'll want to date other girls," Liza said slowly.

"You'll want to date, too," he pointed out. "Won't you?"

"Maybe. But I can't imagine wanting to. Not right now," she answered.

He put down his surfboard and took her in his arms. "You're the only one I want," he said as he kissed her tenderly.

After a few moments they walked down the dirt road toward the beach. "I'll need a picture of you to hang on my wall," she said.

"I'll get you one," he promised. "Poster size."

On the beach, they put down their blanket and continued talking about the upcoming separation.

They agreed that it didn't have to be the end of them. Liza wanted to believe they could make it work. She was glad Eddie felt the same way.

They were still talking when Lloyd and Bruce arrived with their surfboards.

"Let me at those waves," said Lloyd. "I love my job, but boy, do I miss surfing."

"Lead on, O mighty Surf Master," said Bruce with an elaborate hand gesture. "The ocean hasn't been the same since you left it."

"Everything changes," said Lloyd philosophically. "Except surfing."

"Very deep," Eddie said, laughing. "Let's go."

Eddie surfed with them while Liza paged through a fashion magazine. There was a section on coats and hats for the winter. Liza studied it closely. She'd never owned a winter coat in her life.

Liza looked up from her magazine and looked out to the ocean. She could see the three boys surfing. *Everything changes, except surfing.* Ridiculous as it sounded, maybe Lloyd had a point, she thought. Everything was changing. But she would always hold this picture of the boys surfing out on the ocean—so free and wild—inside of her.

Chapter Fourteen

The next week went by for Liza in a blur of activity. She had to sign out of school, shop, pack and give her notice at the Palm Pavilion.

She planned to work right up until the last Saturday. "I'll need every drop of spending money I can get," she told her mother. On Sunday her parents would drive her to the airport in Miami. There she would get a flight directly to New York. Cousin Frieda had promised to meet her at Kennedy Airport in New York.

On Saturday morning Chris came by on her bike, as usual. "I can't believe this is your last day," she said as Liza came out the front door. "It seems like any other day."

"It doesn't seem real to me, either," agreed Liza, getting on her bike. "This morning I woke up and had the funny feeling that I had dreamt the whole thing. Then I saw the airline tickets on my dresser and I knew it was real."

They rode to Sam's house. Mr. O'Neill was loading up his Captain Dan's Snorkeling Tours van. "Here comes our future star," he greeted Liza.

"I hope so," Liza said.

He opened the van's front door and took something off the dashboard. "I saw this on the beach the other day, and I thought of you." He handed her a small dried starfish. "You can hang this on your door when you get to be a big star," he said, laughing.

Liza held the small starfish in her hand. "I will," she promised.

Sam came out onto the porch with Trevor trailing behind her. Mrs. O'Neill and Greta were there, too.

"I have a little something for our wandering girl," said Mrs. O'Neill. She came down off the porch and gave Liza a package wrapped in shocking pink.

"Thanks," said Liza, pulling off the paper. It was a pretty tapestry travel cosmetics bag. Inside were pink tubes of Miss Belle lipstick, eye makeup, blush, mascara and different creams. "These are great," said Liza.

"All the colors should go with your natural coloring. I matched you on the Miss Belle color chart," said Mrs. O'Neill.

"Mom's selling Miss Belle now," Greta told Liza.

Sam rolled her eyes. Her mother was always into some new money-making plan. They had a garage full of house cleaners and Chompy Pet dog food, the results of her last two failed ventures.

Liza looked at the pale pinkish orange lipstick. "This is pretty," she said. "I bet a lot of people will buy it."

"Look at the name on the bottom," said Mrs. O'Neill. "It's called Coral Beach. I figured it would make you think of us."

Liza felt a lump rise in her throat, but she pushed it back. "Thanks, this is real nice." She kissed Mrs. O'Neill, Greta and Mr. O'Neill.

Just then, Lloyd came flying out the front door. "Come on, Greta," he said. "I'm going to be late for work. Did you know that punctuality is the virtue of kings? Mr. Parker told me that."

He hurried past everyone on his way to Greta's Mustang. "I'm coming, Lloyd," called Greta, hurrying after him.

As Greta's car banged into gear, Mr. O'Neill shook his head. "Is Lloyd really that eager to go to work—or is he pulling my leg since I was the one who badgered him into getting a job?" he asked.

"I don't know, Dad," said Sam, getting onto her bike. "You can never tell with Lloyd."

The girls rode to the Palm. As Liza punched her card into the time clock she could hardly believe she was doing it for the last time. She listened to the clatter of pots in the kitchen and watched the white-jacketed cooks, wanting to remember everything about the kitchen. She saw Chef Alleyne, his wild red hair tucked up into his chef's hat, as he bellowed orders to his assistants. He felt her eyes on him and looked up. *"Au revoir, ma petite,"* he said, blowing her a kiss. "Until we meet again."

"Au revoir, Chef Alleyne," Liza replied.

"How did he know I was leaving?" Liza asked as the girls hurried through the Oceana Room.

"I guess the word is out," Chris answered with a shrug.

Out in the lobby, the hotel was bustling. It was the height of the season, and everyone seemed to be moving double-time. Liza, Sam and Chris checked the assignment board.

Liza smiled when she found her name. She was assigned to play checkers with Mr. Schwartz. Liza had planned to see him and say good-bye today. This was even better. She knew they could have used her as a baby sitter. Mrs. Chan had given her this assignment as a going-away present.

Liza had the board set up before Mr. Schwartz arrived. It seemed to her that he looked older than ever as she watched him approach, leaning on his cane, his white pants flapping around his skinny legs. Mrs. Chan met him in the lobby and pointed to Liza.

His eyes lit up with delight. "I was wondering what they rang me up for." He chuckled as he took his seat across the table. "Isn't this a nice surprise."

"Mr. Schwartz," Liza began. "There's no way I can ever thank you for—"

The old man rapped his cane on the floor. "Darn it! Are we here to talk or to play checkers?"

"Checkers," said Liza, suppressing a small smile.

"Good," he said. He moved his black piece out onto the board. "Your move."

They played checkers for hours. After a few games, Mr. Schwartz began giving Liza advice. "And don't let some little, snotty girls scare you off. There are always a few starlets who think they're hot stuff. Real talent will shine. Look at Bette Davis, Claudette Colbert, Kate Hepburn—Myrna Loy. The cream always rises to the top."

Liza didn't dismiss anything he said. She knew he was speaking from years of experience.

Finally, it was three o'clock and her shift ended. "Do you have a warm coat?" Mr. Schwartz asked as Liza helped him up from his chair.

"No, but my mother gave me money to buy one in New York," she told him.

"Fine. Get a good sensible coat. The winds blow cold on Broadway," he advised.

"I will," said Liza. She reached up and kissed his bony cheek. "Thank you from the bottom of my heart," she said quickly.

"You're welcome," he replied. For a second she caught sight of the handsome young actor he once had been. Then it was gone. "I'm overdue for my nap," he grumbled. "No wonder I almost lost that last game. Got to go."

Liza watched him hobble off through the lobby. Mr. Schwartz never lost at checkers. She never let him.

"Ready to go?" asked Sam, joining Liza.

"I'm pooped," said Chris. "That kid I got today was a little menace."

"Come on," Sam said. "Let's get going while we still have some of Saturday left."

"Wait," said Liza. "I want to say good-bye to some people."

"You'd better punch out first," Chris reminded her. "You know Parker. No chitchatting on company time."

"Okay," Liza agreed. They headed into the Oceana Room on their way to the time clock.

"Surprise!" came a chorus of voices.

Liza jumped back, her hand over her rapidly beating heart. There stood Mrs. Chan, Mr. Parker, Raoul Smith the bartender, Lillian and Sunny—even Jannette. There were also waiters, waitresses, bus boys and girls, maids and other staff members with whom Liza had been friendly. Bruce Johnson was there with some of the other pool assistants. Lloyd stood beside Julie, the head lifeguard.

"One, two, three—" Lloyd counted. With that, the staff broke into a rousing chorus of "Give My Regards to Broadway." Liza heard Mr. Parker's beautiful clear voice rising above the others.

114

"This is so great!" Liza said, her eyes filling with happy tears.

Before she could say more, the door to the kitchen swung open and Chef Alleyne wheeled out a sheet cake. He was followed by his assistant cooks. "Chef Alleyne's finest chocolate cake to send you on your way," the chef announced.

"I'm going to miss you all so much," said Liza. "This is so nice of you."

Sam and Chris reached under the table and pulled out a very large gift-wrapped box. "We all chipped in," Chris said, handing the box to Liza.

"I don't believe this," said Liza, tearing the paper. "Oh, my gosh!" she cried when she opened the box. She lifted out a long, royal-blue wool coat with black velvet trim on the collar. "It's beautiful," she said, slipping it on. "It fits, too. And it's so warm."

"We ordered it from a catalog because we couldn't find a single coat around here," Sam told her. "No one could decide which coat to get. Mr. Schwartz convinced us to get this one. He said it was a star's coat."

"That's why he told me to buy a sensible coat," Liza said with a laugh. "He knew I would be getting this gorgeous one."

"And we ordered you something just from us," said Chris. She handed Liza another, smaller box. Inside was a matching blue hat with soft, fake blue fur around the face. Tucked beside that were a pair of black leather gloves.

Liza put them on and looked at her reflection in the glass of one of the paintings on the wall. The outfit was wonderful. And this made it all seem real. She was going to New York!

"Cake," said Mrs. Chan, dishing out the cake Chef Alleyne had cut into slices. The staff began to eat and pour themselves sodas that had been set out on a table.

One by one they came up to Liza and wished her well. Finally Mr. Parker approached.

Liza knew how much she owed him. "Thank you for everything you've done for me," she said. "I'll never forget your help."

"Not at all, Miss Velez," he replied. "And remember, on duty or off, you are always a member of the Palm Pavilion staff. We expect you to act as such."

"I will," said Liza.

Mr. Parker extended his hand. "Good luck, my dear. Now, if you'll excuse me, I believe the guests in Eleven-C are in the midst of some crisis relating to a nonfunctioning air conditioner." As Liza had seen him do a hundred times, Mr. Parker hurried off, his head bent toward the next business at hand.

Liza knew she would never meet anyone like Mr. Parker. Not in New York or anywhere. She missed him already.

Chris came up and put her arm around Liza. "'You are always a member of the Palm Pavilion staff,'" she said, giggling.

"Think of that," said Sam, joining them. "No matter where we go, what we do, we're Palm staffers for life. Do you think people will be able to tell?"

"Probably." Liza laughed. "But you know what else we're going to be for life?"

"What?" asked Sam.

Liza put her arms around their shoulders. "The very best of friends in the whole world."

"That's for sure," Chris agreed.

The three girls hugged tightly, their foreheads pressed together. Liza knew that no matter where they went, they would be together—connected by friendship, forever.

SUZANNE WEYN

Suzanne Weyn is the author of many books for children and young adults. Among them are: *The Makeover Club, Makeover Summer* and the series NO WAY BALLET. Suzanne began baby-sitting at the age of thirteen. Later, while attending Harpur College, she worked as a waitress in a hotel restaurant. Suzanne grew up on Long Island, N.Y., and loves the beach. Sailing, snorkeling, water-skiing and swimming are some of her favorite activities. In SITTING PRETTY she is able to draw on these experiences.

Suzanne now has a baby of her own named Diana, who has two terrific baby sitters—Chris and Joy-Ann.